Tony Zavaleta

Oscar Casares was born and raised in Brownsville, Texas. His stories have appeared in *The Threepenny Review, Northwest Review, Colorado Review,* and *The Iowa Review.* A graduate of the Iowa Writers' Workshop, he has received the Dobie-Paisano Fellowship from the Texas Institute of Letters and the University of Texas, and the James Michener Award from the Copernicus Society of America. He lives in San Antonio and is working on his first novel.

Brownsville

Brownsville

Oscar Casares

BACK BAY BOOKS
LITTLE, BROWN

Little, Brown and Company
Boston · New York · London

FIRST EDITION

Grateful acknowledgment is made to the following publications in which some of these stories were first published:
"Yolanda," *The Threepenny Review;* "Jerry Fuentes," *Northwest Review.*

Library of Congress Cataloging-in-Publication Data

Casares, Oscar.
Brownsville: stories / Oscar Casares. — 1st ed.
p. cm.
ISBN 0-316-14680-3
1. Brownsville (Tex.) — Fiction. 2. Mexican American Border Region — Fiction. 3. Southwestern States — Fiction. 4. Mexican Americans — Fiction. 5. Working class — Fiction. I. Title.

PS3603.A83 B76 2003
813'.6 — dc21

2002026293

10 9 8 7 6 5 4 3

Q-FF

Book design by Fearn Cutler de Vicq
Printed in the United States of America

Para mis padres,

Everardo y Severa Casares

The author wishes to thank the Texas Institute of Letters
and the University of Texas at Austin for the Dobie-Paisano Fellowship,
and the Copernicus Society of America
for the James Michener Award.

Contents

I Thought You and Me Were Friends

Mr. Z

The boy rode in the car with his father. It was late afternoon and they were on their way to buy fireworks. The father had worked a full day and was tired, but he had promised to drive his son to the stands. This was the Fourth of July. They had made the short trip to the edge of town for as long as the boy could remember in his eleven years. He had two older sisters, but they had never enjoyed doing this with their father. When the boy was little, his father lit the fireworks on the sidewalk as the boy watched from the porch with his mother. He would let go of his mother's hand and clap at each small explosion as if he had forgotten the one that had gone off only a minute earlier. Now that he was older, he lit the fireworks with other boys from the neighborhood and sometimes his father stood on the porch to watch.

The fireworks stands were just beyond the city limits sign for Brownsville, Texas. The long and narrow wooden structures were scattered along the dry edges of the highway like giant matches that had fallen from the sky. Behind the stands, the flat sorghum fields stretched for a couple of miles until they reached the Rio Grande. The father stopped next to a stand with a large sign that read MR. Z'S FIREWORKS. The owner of the business introduced himself to the father and they shook hands. "Juan Zamarripa, para servirle," the owner said. Then it was the boy's turn to shake hands. "Diego Morales, sir," he said. The owner was an old man and he wore a red baseball cap with the words MR. Z'S FIREWORKS stenciled across the front. His long white sideburns reminded Diego of cotton strands glued to brown construction paper. On his right forearm the owner had a faded tattoo of an eagle. The two men spoke in Spanish while Diego picked out fireworks. A teenage boy who worked behind the counter helped him. After his father paid for the fireworks, the owner motioned for Diego to come closer.

"I think you forgot something," the old man said as he dropped an extra bottle rocket inside the bag.

"What do you say?" the father was quick to ask.

"Thank you," Diego said.

The old man nodded. "How old are you, son?"

"Eleven."

"Eleven?" the old man said. "N'hombre, by the time I was your age I had a job and my own money. Are you good in math?"

"Yes, sir."

"Vamos a ver, let's say I buy three dollars and fifty cents' worth of fireworks and I give you a five-dollar bill. What's my change?"

"One dollar and fifty cents," Diego said.

"Hey, you're faster than some people I know," Mr. Z said and glanced at the boy behind the counter. "You should come work for me, son. I don't pay a lot, but you get all your fireworks for fifty percent off."

Diego looked up at his father.

"If you want the job, you can have it," his father said.

"Bueno, I have enough help right now," Mr. Z said. "But I'll call you before New Year's and let's see what we can do."

That night Diego popped his fireworks in the street with the other neighborhood boys, but he couldn't stop thinking about what had happened earlier that day. He thought of all the other jobs in the world he could have, and none of them were as great as working at a fireworks stand. His sisters didn't even have jobs yet. They were always asking for money to go out with their friends. And now he would be earning enough to buy his own fireworks. Who knew how much he could buy if they were only half price? He told his friends, and some of the older boys wanted to know if they needed more help at the stand. He told them he couldn't say, but he would let them know. The dark sky flashed before him in brilliant colors and New Year's seemed as if it would take forever to get here.

The summer and autumn months passed slowly until Mr. Z phoned Diego the second week of December.

"Are you still interested, son?"

"Yes, sir."

"And you're willing to work hard?"

"Oh, yes, sir."

"That's good, because the boys I hired last summer were lazy. They started off okay, but they got lazy on me."

"I'll work hard. I'm not lazy."

"I didn't think you were. Your father doesn't look like a lazy man."

"No, sir."

"Bueno, we're opening next week, a few days before Christmas, and going all the way to New Year's. My boys come in at noon and work late. How does that sound to you?"

"It sounds good. All my friends, they wish they could work at your stand."

"That's good to hear, son," the old man said. "You stop by next Wednesday and I'll show you how we work at Mr. Z's. Tell your father I can give you a ride home when we close down."

Diego spent the next few days wishing that he could be at work already. It was a good thing he didn't have to share a room the way his sisters did. He wanted to be alone. He heard his parents talking the night before he started. His mother thought he was too young to be working until the stand closed, but his father said Diego had already promised the man he would work. His boy was not going to back out now. He wouldn't let her treat him like a baby. They were quiet after that. Diego fell asleep wondering how different his life would be if tomorrow ever came.

His father drove home at lunch the next day. He wanted to take his son to his first day of work. Diego had spent some time getting ready that morning. After he showered, he brushed his teeth and put on his favorite blue jeans. He used a few drops of his father's Tres Flores to comb his hair. When they heard the car horn, Diego's mother kissed him on the cheek and told him to be careful. He said okay and ran to the car where his father was waiting.

They cracked the windows open at the top to let in the cool air. The sky was ash gray, as it had been for the past week. On the way to the stands they passed the cafés along International Boulevard, the panadería and its glorious scent of fresh sweet bread, the restaurant that sold barbacoa on Sunday mornings, the service station where the father had worked as a young man.

"You need to pay attention to Mr. Zamarripa," his father said. "Don't be playing around with the other boys. I want you to be serious. ¿Me entiendes?"

"Yes, sir."

These were the only words they exchanged on the way to the stand, but Diego knew what his father meant. He wanted Diego to behave and not do anything to embarrass him in front of Mr. Z. The tone of his father's voice was serious. It was the same tone he used right before he got angry. Once, his father had told him to be careful with the orange soda he was drinking in the car and then a minute later, when the soda spilled on the cloth seats, his father slapped him. His father had hit him a couple of other times, enough for Diego to know that tone of voice. When they arrived at the stand, his father stayed in the car and waved to Mr. Z. "Pay attention," he said.

Another boy was inside the stand with Mr. Z. His name was Ricky and he had also been hired to work. Although they were about the same age, he was shorter and huskier than Diego. Ricky lived in the projects near Diego's house, but they had never met.

It was warmer inside the stand and Diego put away the windbreaker his mother had made him wear. The old man handed each of the boys a red MR. Z'S FIREWORKS cap. They thanked him and put them on. Diego was too busy adjusting the size to notice that his cap was bent and the brim was worn down and dirty.

"Bueno, I'm going to tell you what we got here at Mr. Z's. Black Cats is the most popular firecracker there is." The old man showed them the black and red package. "You got no Black Cats, you got no New Year's. It's my all-time bestseller. Nobody beats El Gato Negro." He raised his hands as if they were claws. The boys backed up.

"These are the Black Snakes. You light the fuse and it starts smoking and a tiny snake comes out — these are good for the little kids. Sparklers, too. If a man comes in alone, he probably has kids at home. And, Diego, what do you offer him?"

"Black Snakes and sparklers."

"That's right, son. Now you're using what God gave you," the old man said and pointed to Diego's head. "Over here are the smoke bombs, another bestseller. Who doesn't like smoke bombs?"

The boys stared at the old man.

"Who?" he said.

"Nobody?" Ricky said.

"Good answer," Mr. Z said. "The older kids go for bottle rockets, guaranteed. Roman candles are Roman candles. If you don't know what those are, you're in the wrong business. Silver Jets are new. They make a loud sound like a coffeepot when it's ready. Every pinche perro in the neighborhood barks when they hear it take off. It's for the big kids."

The boys listened to Mr. Z explain how to sell some of the less-popular fireworks, place the money in a tin box under the counter, and bag everything the customers bought. He covered the stand from one end to the other. Diego already knew all the fireworks because he'd been buying them for years, but he didn't want to tell the old man this and be disrespectful.

When Mr. Z finished, he left the boys in the stand and walked to his pale yellow truck. He had parked it a few yards beyond the stand, the front end pointed into the ditch. There was a camper on the bed that looked rustier than the ancient truck it was attached to. The old man sat in the driver's seat for a long stretch of time. He finally walked to the front of the stand to watch the boys help some customers. After the people drove away, he brought Diego and Ricky together.

"Diego, what's the matter? How come you don't smile more? Who wants to buy fireworks from somebody who's got a serious face?"

"I don't know."

"You need to smile, son. Right now you look like you're going to the rest room, making number two." The old man strained his face and pretended he was sitting on a toilet.

Ricky laughed. So did Diego, but then he remembered what his father had said and he tried to be serious again.

"Y tú, Ricky, what are you laughing at?" Mr. Z said. "Didn't I tell you to sell the Black Snakes to the men who come in alone?"

"Yes, sir."

"¿Entonces? What happened with that last man with the red shirt?"

"I forgot."

"*I forgot.* You better not *forgot* next time."

The boys did better with the people who stopped by the rest of that afternoon. Mr. Z kept walking behind the customers and exaggerating his smile to make Diego remember what he had said. Ricky sold three packages of sparklers and Black Snakes.

At four o'clock, Mr. Z said it was time for dinner. If they waited until five or six, there would be too many customers. He asked the boys what they wanted from Whataburger.

"I didn't bring enough money," Diego said.

"You don't need no money. I pay for all the meals my boys eat. You just tell me what you want."

Mr. Z brought back three cheeseburgers, fries, and drinks. They sat on the tailgate of the truck and looked at the passing cars and trucks. The boys wouldn't get paid for another week, so the meal was a small reward. Diego liked working hard. His father worked hard as a mechanic, sometimes taking side jobs to bring in a little extra. On those weekends, two or three cars would be parked in the backyard, waiting to be repaired. Diego took another bite. He thought this had to be the best cheeseburger he ever tasted.

The stand closed at ten o'clock. Mr. Z counted the money while the boys swept the inside of the stand and locked the doors and windows. Ricky had ridden his ten-speed bike to work, but Mr. Z told him to put it in the back of the truck because he was giving them both a ride home.

The old man used his hand to sweep the crumpled newspapers, used bags of chicharrones, soda cans, and Mexican lottery tickets from the passenger's seat onto the floor. Diego sat in the middle and Ricky leaned against the door. A tiny hula girl was glued to the dashboard. The boys watched her grass skirt swish around each time the truck hit a bump in the road.

"You two remind me of my boys." The old man pulled out a black-and-white photo that was clipped to the sun visor. "Mira, aquí están, when they were still in the hospital."

He turned on the cab light to show them the photo of the twin babies. Their faces were scrunched together and they were both crying.

"What do you think? Do they look like their old man?"

"Kind of," Ricky said.

"What do they look like now?" Diego handed back the photo and Mr. Z put it in his shirt pocket.

"You have to ask their mama that question. She left to Chicago when they were still babies." The old man was quiet for a while, looking at the truck's headlights on the road. "But if they're my boys, they're probably some handsome men now," he said and laughed a little.

They were at the Four Corners intersection when the old man opened the glove box. Some receipts fell out and he grabbed a quart of whiskey. The bottle had a picture of a fighting cock on the label. Mr. Z took a quick drink and handed the bottle to Diego.

"Andale, you got to drink to your first day of work. It was a good day, we made some good money," the old man said.

Diego winced as soon as he tasted the whiskey. He wanted to spit it out, but he drank it instead.

"You too, Ricky. Today you're workingmen, hombres trabajadores."

Diego was glad that the old man held on to the bottle for the rest of the ride.

His mother and father were waiting for him in the living room. His sisters came out of their room when they heard him walk in the door.

"How was your first day?" his father said.

"Are you hungry, mi'jito?" his mother said.

She reheated some tamales, and the family crowded around him at the kitchen table.

"So, Diego, are you going to lend us money now?" his oldest sister asked and laughed.

"You girls leave your brother alone — he's eating," his father said.

When Diego finished his meal, he told them about learning how to work inside the stand and eating cheeseburgers on the tailgate of the truck and selling fireworks to little kids and going to the rest room behind a mesquite and almost seeing a wreck between an 18-wheeler and a car that pulled out onto the highway too fast and cleaning the place after they closed. He told them everything, except the part about the ride home and the bottle with the rooster on it.

The next day Diego made it to work before Ricky. He took care of the few customers that came by early. Mr. Z kept looking at his watch and shaking his head. At one point, the old man wrote something in the little notepad that he used to record all the sales for the day.

Diego was rearranging the bottle rockets when Ricky finally showed up for work. His mother had driven him to the stand. Diego noticed she was a lot younger than most of his friends' moms. She wore large hoop earrings and her dark hair was in a ponytail. She apologized to Mr. Z for Ricky being an hour late. Someone had stolen his bike. Ricky's eyes were swollen as though he had been crying.

"It won't happen again," she promised.

"No te preocupes por eso," Mr. Z assured her. "I'm sorry you had to bring Ricky all this way. I would've been happy to pick him up."

Mr. Z walked her to the car and he stood talking to her for a couple of minutes until she drove away. He was smiling when he came back to the stand.

"Why didn't you tell me your mother was such a beautiful woman, eh, Ricky? And alone, without a man? I thought you and me were friends."

Ricky looked at the ground.

"N'hombre, if I didn't have a business to run, I might have taken the afternoon off." The old man laughed.

Diego tried to turn away, but the old man looked straight at him.

"That's a joke, son — laugh. I thought you were going to smile more."

Diego gave him a half smile, but Mr. Z only turned his back and walked to the truck. Ricky was quiet, and Diego felt bad for even trying to smile. He didn't understand why Mr. Z was talking about Ricky's mom. At school you didn't talk about anybody's mother or sister. There was a boy in class who wrote some bad words in the rest room about a girl named Letty, and her four brothers jumped him on the way home, near the canal by the church. The brothers took turns kicking him in the stomach and head.

Later in the afternoon, Mr. Z bought a family box of fried chicken and biscuits.

"Is your mother a good cook, Ricky?" the old man asked.

"I guess so."

"Nothing like a beautiful woman who can cook."

"My father barbecues in the backyard," Diego said. "My tío Lalo, he's my uncle who was in the navy, he comes over and they make chicken and fajitas, and sometimes they throw beer on the fire to make it . . ." He stopped when he saw the old man glare at him as if he had a piece of food hanging out of his mouth. He realized that Mr. Z didn't want to be interrupted. No one said anything. They ate the rest of the chicken and listened to the passing cars on the highway.

On the ride home, Mr. Z opened a new bottle of whiskey and turned the radio to a Tejano station. The old man knew the song and was swaying a little in his seat. Ricky looked out the window. Diego watched the hula girl's skirt. When they were in front of his apartment, Ricky swung the truck door open.

"Tell your mother good night for me, eh, Ricky?"

The boy just walked away. The old man drove to Diego's house.

"What do you think, Diego?" he said.

"About what, sir?"

"Is she a good-looking woman, or is a she good-looking woman?"

"I don't know, sir."

"That wasn't one of the choices, son."

They stopped in front of Diego's house.

"Thank you for the ride, Mr. Z."

The old man gunned the engine and took off.

The next day, Diego and his father drove by Ricky's apartment and gave him a ride to work. Mr. Z looked surprised to see both boys getting out of the car.

"Eh, Ricky, why didn't you tell me you needed a ride?" the old man said. "I would've stopped by your house."

"It's okay, Diego said his father could give me a ride."

"And who the hell is his father? You don't work for his father." The old man stared at the boys until they looked away.

Diego thought he was helping out by giving Ricky a ride to work. Now he felt sorry that he had somehow made things worse.

The boys restocked the displays. They placed everything in the same position it had been in the past two days, the best-sellers in the front and the less-popular fireworks on either side of them. An hour passed before the old man stood in front of the stand to watch the boys work. Ricky was helping Diego sell more fireworks to a man who had driven up alone.

"The best one for little kids are the Black Snakes," Ricky said. "They're safe because there's no popping and that way there's no chance of getting hurt. All you do is light the fuse and a little snake comes out."

"Yeah, they come out like the rattlesnakes do on the King Ranch," Diego said. He thought it was a clever way to explain what they actually did.

The man added two packages of Black Snakes to the fireworks he was buying.

Mr. Z walked inside the stand after the customer left.

"Diego, how come you told that man a lie?"

"What do you mean?"

"Rattlesnakes," the old man said. "There no rattlesnakes on the King Ranch. I've hunted there, lots of times. I've never seen rattlesnakes."

"My father told me there was."

"Then your father lied. Your father told you some bullshit."

"He's never lied to me."

"You're calling me a liar?"

"No, sir."

"¿Entonces?"

"Nothing, sir."

"Bueno, you better watch what you say to people or you're going to turn out the same as your father, a bullshitter."

Diego didn't know what to say. He wanted to be angry with Mr. Z, but he also wondered if he should apologize for arguing with him about the snakes.

Mr. Z walked back to the truck. He stayed there for the rest of the afternoon. When he left to buy dinner, the boys stood in front of the fireworks stand and threw pebbles into the ditch.

"I bet there are rattlesnakes at the King Ranch," Ricky said.

"That's what my father says," Diego said.

"Don't listen to the old man. He's just mad because my mom didn't bring me."

"My father doesn't lie."

"I know. You don't have to tell me."

Mr. Z brought fried chicken again. The boys each grabbed a piece with a paper napkin. They looked out at the cars driving past them. The sun was burning on the horizon and it would be dark soon.

"How's the chicken today, boys?"

"It's good," Diego said.

Ricky nodded.

"You know, people tell me that snake tastes like chicken," the old man said. "What do you think, Diego?"

"Maybe."

"What do you think your father would say about that?"

"I don't know."

"Really? I thought your tío would come over to the house and barbecue snakes."

"No, sir."

"Ahh, I think you forgot, Diego," the old man said. "Maybe I should ask your father myself. He probably has some good ways to barbecue a snake."

A family in a white van stopped next to the truck, and Diego put away his food to help them. He stayed in the stand for the rest of the night. They were busy that evening and the old man didn't have time to say anything to him.

After work he made sure to sit next to the passenger door, where he wouldn't have to hear as much of Mr. Z talking. His father was watching the late news when Diego walked in and sat next to him on the sofa.

"How was it today, mi'jo?" his father asked.

"It was okay."

"Good. Are you paying attention to Mr. Zamarripa?"

"Yes, sir."

"Are you going to college so you can study to be a businessman?"

"Maybe," Diego said. "But I'm kind of getting tired of selling fireworks."

"You been working three days, Diego. You don't know what tired is."

"But we're not even getting paid until the last day."

"It's only one more week. Just be glad you have a job. ¿Me entiendes?" His father was serious now.

"Yes, sir."

They watched the weather report for a few minutes. His father wanted to see if there was going to be a cold front.

"Dad, remember last year when we drove by the King Ranch?"

His father nodded.

"And remember how you told me there were rattlesnakes all over the ranch?"

"Yeah."

"Have you seen them?"

"No, mi'jo, but I can imagine there are lots of them. Why?"

"Mr. Z goes hunting there and he's never seen one."

"Pues, maybe he's right. I'm not a hunter."

Diego had trouble sleeping that night. What his father had said about the rattlesnakes didn't sound like a lie, but it wasn't exactly the truth, either. He thought about how it might be possible to imagine something and for it to be true. Diego wished there were an easy way of telling his father what had happened. Explaining it to his mother wouldn't help. His father would find out and he'd have to tell him everything, straight to his face. Diego pictured himself trying to say what Mr. Z had said, and he knew he couldn't embarrass his father that way. Even if he was only repeating the words, it was still an insult. He hated the old man for saying his father was a liar. And he hated the fact that he couldn't quit his job.

Diego's father dropped him and Ricky off at work. Mr. Z met the boys in front of the stand. They watched Diego's father wave as he drove away.

The old man was the first to wave back. "Come on, boys, say good-bye to the bullshitter."

The words stung Diego like a fresh scab being torn from his arm. The rest of the day was filled with Mr. Z making jokes about Diego's father, about how he'd make a good politician, about how he could fool one of those lie-detector machines, about how he probably lied all the time, even to Diego's mother.

The old man left to buy dinner at the usual time. Diego told Ricky he was going to the rest room. Then he sat behind a mesquite and cried. He held the loose dirt in his hand and it slipped through his fingers. There was nothing he wanted more than to be older and be able to talk back to the old man. He didn't know what he would say, but he wanted to hurt him. Maybe he could set the stand on fire and ruin his business. Diego could see himself going to jail for this, and he thought it would be worth it. If he were bigger, he would've fought him and knocked him to the ground. He'd hit the old man hard, maybe knock out a tooth. There would be tears in his eyes and blood dripping from his mouth. Diego would keep kicking him in the stomach until he begged him to stop. People passing by in cars would laugh. And he'd slap him with the back of his hand one more time, just to make sure the old man knew he had done wrong.

Mr. Z and Ricky were sitting on the tailgate. Diego wiped his eyes and runny nose on the inside of his shirt. He walked to the truck and started eating his cheeseburger. All the crying had left a funny taste in his mouth and he wasn't that hungry.

He was eating his french fries when two young boys came by on a bike, one of them sitting on the handlebars. Diego said he'd take care of them.

The boys were brothers and their hair was cut the same way, in a straight line across their forehead. Diego brought out the sparklers and Black Snakes, but they weren't interested in little-kid fireworks. One brother wanted bottle rockets and the other wanted Silver Jets.

"Bottle rockets are stupid," the younger one said.

"No, they're not," the older one said.

"I'm sick of bottle rockets."

"Stop being a llorón. Bottle rockets is all we got money for. The Silver Jets cost more."

"You're the llorón. You're the one that wants bottle rockets. Those are for stupid babies. Give me half the money."

They argued for several minutes, calling each other names. The younger one kicked dirt at his brother, which led to a shoving match the older one eventually won. In the end, they bought two packages of bottle rockets.

The boys were still arguing when Diego dropped four Silver Jets in their paper bag without them noticing. He did it as if it were the most natural thing in the world to do, as if he were standing in the middle of the street lighting the fuse to a long pack of Black Cats.

The brothers rode away with their fireworks, and Diego wished he could see their reaction when they found the Silver Jets. He felt himself kicking the old man in the gut.

Later Diego helped a man wearing a black cowboy hat

with a tiny horseshoe pin stuck to the front of it. The man bought Roman candles, bottle rockets, Silver Jets, and Black Cats. Diego put them all inside a paper bag and then slipped in two more Roman candles. If the man noticed, he didn't say anything. Diego charged him only for the fireworks he had asked for. The man nodded and walked to his truck.

Diego gave away fireworks every chance he had. The packages of Black Snakes, smoke bombs, bottle rockets, Black Cats, and sparklers tumbled to the bottom of the paper bags for the rest of the night. It became a game for him, a challenge, the same way learning how to sell Black Snakes and sparklers had been a challenge. The trick was to figure out what kind of firework the customer really wanted and to stick it in the bag without anyone noticing. A heavyset lady with three kids almost caught him putting some extra smoke bombs in her bag.

"¿Y ésos, qué? Are you trying to trick me, make me buy more than I want?"

"No, ma'am, these are two for one."

"¿Estás seguro? Because I don't like tricks."

"Yes, ma'am, they're on special."

"Pues, entonces let me buy two more de esos smoke bombs."

He had started by giving away the fireworks only when he was alone in the stand, but with the evening rush he became more daring. With Ricky working next to him and Mr. Z at the other end of the counter with a customer, he dropped the fireworks in a bag and then smiled at the old man as if he'd just made the biggest sale of the night.

Mr. Z told more of his jokes on the ride home. The one he

laughed at the most was about how Diego's father probably
never went to confession because it would take too long.
Ricky ignored the old man and stared straight ahead as if he
were on a long bus ride. Diego sat next to the door. It was
colder now, but he rolled down the window because he didn't
want to hear the jokes. He wondered what would happen in
a day or two when the old man did an inventory check. It
was the first time he had thought about it all night. Each time
he had added extra fireworks to a customer's bag, he felt he
was somehow covering up the last time he had done it, so
that in the end it wouldn't be dozens of fireworks that had
been given away but only one or two packages that could
easily be written off as a mistake. It became less of a bad
thing the more he did it. Now he was getting nervous that
one of his customers would come back to ask Mr. Z for free
fireworks, telling him that one of his boys had been loading
up bags the night before. He was afraid Ricky might get
blamed, and then he would have to come forward and confess
the whole thing. Given the choice, he would prefer to get fired
and not have to confess. He didn't feel bad about what he had
done, because the old man deserved everything, maybe more.
In the distance, fireworks lit up the dark sky, and Diego imagined they were the Roman candles he'd given away. He
smiled as he watched the bright lights.

When Diego opened the front door, he saw his father
drinking a glass of water in the kitchen. He had hoped that
his parents might already be asleep. He wanted to go to bed
without having to talk about his day, but as soon as he
walked in, his father asked him to sit at the table.

"How was work, mi'jo?"

Diego hesitated for a moment. He stared at the salt and pepper shakers on the table, trying to find an answer in the grains.

"It was good," he said. "I think I sold more fireworks than anybody."

"That's the kind of news I like to hear about my boy."

Diego smiled.

"Then you're going to keep working for Mr. Zamarripa?"

"Yes, sir."

"Qué bueno," his father said. "I knew everything would work out. Sometimes you just have to wait a little while for it to get better."

RG

I saw Bannert at the mall the other day. He was standing near the entrance eating a cone of pistachio ice cream. He pretended he didn't see me, and I returned the favor. This is the same man who used to live across the street from us years ago. Our boys grew up together, played, got into fights. Bannert would wave hello if we happened to pull out of our driveways at the same time. He knows a little bit of Spanish, and sometimes when he came over to the house he tried to say a few words here and there. I appreciated the effort he made. If we saw each other at one of the high school football games, we might shake hands. We were never close friends, but there was a time when we talked in the way neighbors do. That was years ago, though. I couldn't find anything to say to him that day at the mall. And I guess the same goes for him.

Bannert probably thinks I'm crazy. But I'm not. I can tell you exactly when the trouble started — October 3, 1976. I know the date because I keep a record of things. It's nothing fancy, not a diary or anything like that. I just write down what I do every day. It started when I was delivering bread and I had a problem with my supervisor. One day I noticed he was following me on my route, checking to see that I wasn't slacking off. The man had a problem trusting people. He wasn't from around here — maybe that had something to do with it. Either way, I thought writing everything down on paper was a good way to defend myself if he ever said anything against me. I did this at the end of the day, right before I went to bed. Just a few short notes about what I did on my route, the people I spoke to, the mileage on the vehicle, and how long a lunch break I took. Then one night I was writing down all the things I'd done and I realized I hadn't worked that day. This was a Sunday. It had become a habit after so many years, is what I'm trying to say. From then on I wrote in my notebook every night, even after I quit that job and found a better one.

Don't think that I spend a lot of time writing in it, because I don't. Here's what I wrote last Saturday:

Breakfast at Reyna's Cafe, rotated and balanced tires, bought a new ceiling fan, haircut at Treviño's.

If it's a good haircut I might mention it, but usually it's just a haircut. Sometimes I look back at the end of the year and see what I was doing. Or I'll pull out a notebook and see what I was doing five years ago on that day. I have one for every year back to 1973. They're small spiral notebooks, fifty pages, the same ones the kids use in school. I write the year on the cover.

October 3, 1976 — Mowed grass, front and back, trimmed weeds growing next to fence, loaned hammer to Bannert.

So, you see, I have it in writing. I'm not crazy.

My wife said Bannert probably just forgot. I don't know how an honest man forgets for almost four years. I don't know how he wakes up every morning, walks out his front door, looks across the street — straight at my house — and forgets he hasn't returned my hammer.

But she's quick to defend other people, make excuses for them, especially if they happen to have blue eyes. Then they can't go wrong. She thought I was exaggerating the time I told her about my supervisor following me. She claimed that the reason I was so upset was because this supervisor happened to be a gringo. That is her opinion. I've come to expect this from her. You should have seen her when we first moved here. There were only a few Anglo families, but she thought we were living at the country club. Over the years, most of them have moved across town or passed away, until it's come to be almost all raza that live here. I've lived and worked with gringos my whole life. Gringos, mexicanos, negros, chinos. It makes no difference to me. I've always been more interested in living next to honest people than anything else. After that, they can be any color they want.

My wife actually wanted me to walk over and ask Bannert for the hammer.

"Excuse me, Mr. Bannert, but you know that hammer you borrowed a really long time ago, the one you know and I know is mine, pues, I need it back now."

Something like that. But I said I wasn't the one who did the borrowing, so why should I be the one doing the asking?

I was sitting on the porch steps sharpening the blades on the clippers when Bannert came over that afternoon. He stared like he'd never seen anybody sharpen blades. He stared long enough that he made me uncomfortable, and I finally stood up. I don't like people standing over me when I'm working. He was wearing a white T-shirt and a pair of overalls that had creases. His freckled skin was burning with the sun. Bannert isn't the kind of man who works outside every day. He earns his living selling sofas and beds and whatever else they have in a furniture store. If he had yard work, he usually hired somebody to do it.

"The yard looks good, hombre," he said.

"It could use some rain," I said.

"I guess that's why God made sprinklers." He laughed at this.

"Looks like you're getting ready to do some work, Bannert."

"Yeah, I need to fix a few things around la casa. The dryer needs a new exhaust hose. Plus my wife has me hanging up some curtain rods but, chingado, I can't find my hammer. You think I can borrow yours?"

That's how it happened. That's how I remember it, anyway.

He's not the first person I ever loaned something to. George Fuentes used my weed whacker once or twice. I let Domingo, the man who cleans yards, borrow my machete when the handle on his broke loose. Torres needed a small wrench to fix a toilet. Nobody can say I'm pinche with my tools. But then all those things were returned to me within a day, two days at the most.

Bannert was different. Four days went by y nada. No hammer, no apologies, no "Do you mind if I borrow it for a few more days, hombre?" Nothing. Like they say on the radio: Ni-fu, ni-fa.

So I asked myself, "How long do I wait before I say something?"

It's not like he was a stranger who was going to run off the next day. He lived on the other side of the street, maybe a hundred feet from his front door to mine. If I went over too soon, it was going to look like I was desperate and I didn't believe he'd bring the hammer back on his own, which wasn't so far from the truth.

I can only remember one thing that I ever borrowed from Bannert. It wasn't even for me, really. My wife invited some of her family to go with us to the beach and we needed an extra folding table for all the food. We thought Bannert might have one and he did. I put a plastic covering over the table just in case one of our boys spilled something on it. I didn't want Bannert saying later that those people across the street didn't know how to take care of things. And as soon as we got home, I wiped off the sand and returned the table to him. Bannert looked surprised to see me and asked if one of the legs had busted. The man couldn't understand why I wanted to return the table so quickly.

"Thanks," he said, "but you didn't have to bring it back so fast. I knew you'd stop by when you had a chance."

Right there's the difference between us. Bannert takes everything for granted. Why should I have kept his table one minute longer than I needed it? I was glad that he had a table and he was willing to lend it to me in the first place. He thought it was okay to bring back my hammer when it was convenient, when it suited him. I don't work that way.

Time passed: two weeks, three months, seven months, a year, two years.

I understand that most people would've already done something about the hammer, but I'm not most people. I never felt it was my responsibility. Bannert's a grown man. He knew what he was doing. I shouldn't have to go around picking up after him. Just forget about it, my wife said — which was easy to say, since he didn't take something that belonged to her.

During that time, I saw him use my hammer on three different occasions:

May 18, 1977 — Mowed front yard, trimmed grass along the sidewalk, cleaned lawn mower, watched Bannert hammer a new mailbox onto the side of his carport.

*November 30, 1979 — Raked leaves in front and back-
yard, changed oil and filter in car, saw Bannert and his
wife nailing Merry Christmas decorations to the front
of his house.*

*July 4, 1980 — Sprayed tree for worms, washed car, drove
the boys to fireworks stands, Bannert posted a red,
white, and blue sign in his yard: Vote Reagan.*

I'm not a political man, not any more than the next De-
mocrat on this block, but I came pretty close to walking over
there and grabbing the hammer out of his hand. The problem
now was so much time had gone by that saying anything
would make it look like I had been hiding my true feelings
the past four years. That every morning when he waved and
I waved back, I wasn't thinking, "Good morning, Bannert."
That instead I was really thinking, "Why the hell hasn't this
gringo brought back my hammer?" But the truth is that I didn't
think about it all the time. Sometimes months would pass
before I remembered again. And when it did come to mind,
it was more like a leaky faucet that you forget about until
some night when you can't fall asleep and then you hear the
plop . . . plop . . . plop . . . plop . . . but then you forget about
it again the next morning.

I will say that after the first year — when it was clear to
me that he wasn't bringing back the hammer — there were
fewer and fewer reasons to be friendly. He'd wave and I
would nod back, just enough to let him know that I'd seen
him. After mowing the yard, I used to sweep the curb and then
walk over and sweep his side — I figured the street belonged to

the both of us and if his side looked good, my side looked good — but I put an end to that. Christmas Eve we have a tradition of inviting our family and a few neighbors over to the house for tamales. My wife and I were going to sleep after one of these parties and she asked me if I knew why the Bannerts hadn't come. "I guess I forgot to invite them," I said.

I think he got the idea, because he stopped coming around. He stopped being so quick to wave. He stopped bringing fruit-cakes around the holidays, which was fine with me because I never touched them anyway. When he threw a big New Year's party and cars were parked up and down the street, we were somehow not on the invitation list. But as far as I was concerned, he could keep his fruitcakes and his invitations, the same way he'd kept my hammer.

It's not like I stopped hammering altogether. If I needed to replace some shingles on the house or fix the leg on a table, I used my other hammer. It was an older one that had belonged to my father. The handle was wooden and the head was rusty. I had to wrap duct tape on the handle because the wood was splitting. The head rattled when I used it, and I knew it wouldn't be long before it broke off. My other hammer, the one across the street, was all steel with a black rubber grip. It fit in my palm like a firm handshake. I bought it at Sears.

Maybe I should've written my name on it, my initials: RG. But you wouldn't think you'd have to do that with your own hammer. I wasn't working on some construction job where your tools can get lost. It wasn't a suitcase that somebody might pick up by mistake and walk off with. Your hammer should be your hammer, your property. You never know when you're going to need it.

August 5, 1980 — Finished painting the outside trim on the house, cleaned brushes and tray, watched news — weatherman says hurricane headed to the Valley.

We don't get hurricanes every year, but if you lived through Beulah in '67, you know what they can do. It did most of its damage right here and in Matamoros. Trees were ripped out of the ground, phone lines got knocked over, just about every part of the city flooded, the electricity was out for almost a week. All the food and milk in the refrigerator went bad. Forget about clean water. I lost two trees in the backyard. The wind had that poor grapefruit tree twisting around like a pair of underwear hanging on the clothesline. The mesquite split right down the middle. We heard the wood cracking all the way inside the house and I felt a part of me was also being ripped up. The biggest branch fell on the fence and made it into an accordion. And what happened here is nothing compared to what those poor people went through on the other side of the river. Nobody wanted to have that experience again.

There wasn't anything to do but wait. Wait and pray that it died down or turned some other direction. I watched the news every chance I had. Some people were in the habit of leaving the area, driving north, whenever they heard news like this. I can't say I blame them, but it wasn't something we ever did.

> *August 9, 1980 — Hurricane Allen expected to hit Brownsville-Matamoros tonight, weatherman says winds over 170 mph (his words: "could be stronger than Beulah"), took day off from work, bought boards at De Luna Lumber, boarded up windows, Bannert finally gave me back my hammer.*

There's more that I didn't write down in the notebook — there always is.

First of all, let me say that we lived through the hurricane and we're still here today. Me writing in my notebooks, Bannert eating ice cream cones at the mall. The hurricane ended up hitting the coast about forty miles north of here, where there weren't as many people. It still did its damage. It just wasn't as bad as it could have been. A few trees were knocked down on our street and we were without electricity and water for a day, but we survived. Bannert stayed around for a year and then moved to a new subdivision on the north side of town. Four months later another family moved in across from us.

But what sticks out in my mind about the hurricane happened the afternoon before it actually hit. I was waiting in line for almost an hour at De Luna. It looked like half of Brownsville was there buying lumber. Bannert was towards the back of the line, but neither of us made an effort to say hello. The other men were talking about what they'd been through with the last big hurricane. An older man with a cane told everybody how he'd lost a sister in Matamoros when she drowned in her front yard. He said the two boys with him were her children but that he had raised them as if they were his own.

As I stood in line, I could see a policeman directing traffic on International because the lights had gone out. People tried to get in and out of the Lopez Supermarket on that side of the street. My wife was inside there buying all the food and candles she could fit into a shopping cart. The parking lot was full of women loading their cars with enough groceries to wait out the worst of the storm.

I was sliding the last board onto the bed of my truck when I noticed Bannert and one of the De Luna workers unloading a cart stacked with boards. Anybody could tell they weren't going to be able to fit all that lumber in the trunk of Bannert's car, and if they did, he was going to cause an accident. Some other day they might have delivered the boards to his house, but there was a line of men still waiting to buy lumber.

"Looks like you could use some help getting that back to the house, Bannert," I said.

"You have room in your truck?" he asked.

"I think I can fit a few more boards."

We each grabbed an end of the first board and started loading, one by one, neither one of us saying a word. We hadn't talked in almost four years — why start now? He drove out of the parking lot first, and I followed him back to the neighborhood. On the way there, I saw him keeping an eye on me in the rearview mirror like I might forget where he lived. When we were at his house, I backed my truck into the driveway. Again, we grabbed the boards one by one until we had them all leaning against the carport.

"Now I just have to get them up there," he said and laughed.

"Maybe one of your boys can help you."

"Nah, they're still too young. They'd only get in the way."

I thought about his situation and what I should do. He was right about his boys getting in the way. Mine wouldn't be any help, either, but at least I knew I could board up my house without any help. I remember looking at Bannert's overalls, a little faded now, but still with the creases.

"Two can work faster than one," I finally said. "Why don't I help you get started with some of these windows?"

I had my old hammer in the toolbox in my truck. Bannert brought out a stepladder so I could reach the top of the windows. He held the boards against the house and I hammered the nails in. I could hear the sound of banging hammers and the grinding of electric saws coming from every direction. I stopped a couple of times just to listen. I wanted to believe the hammers were somehow sending messages all over the neighborhood. Messages saying what we didn't have words to say ourselves. Regardless of what had happened between us, I didn't mind helping Bannert this one afternoon. His family lived in this neighborhood, just like mine. If I could lend a hand, why not give it? And I had the sense that if he had been in a position to help me with something that he wouldn't have hesitated. That's what I believed. But I also knew we would've never talked if the situation hadn't turned out the way it did. And after this work was done, we would stop talking again. We'd go back to ignoring each other, and that's just the way life would be around here. I knew it even back then.

I ended up doing most of the work that afternoon, but when we were at the last window I thought he might want to do one.

"You want to knock a few in?"

"You bet," he said.

We switched places. I held the board against the window, and Bannert climbed the stepladder. He took a couple of practice swings with the hammer and then hit his first nail. He had two good swings before he hit to the left and the nail bent sideways. It took a couple of taps to straighten it out and start again. The next few nails went the same way.

"Be sure you hit the center of the head and put some more weight behind your swing."

He nodded okay and banged the nail a couple of times. On the next swing he missed the nail altogether and the hammer pounded the side of the house. That was what finally made the head crack off the wooden handle. The head flopped over like a chicken with a broken neck.

"Sorry." He stayed looking at the broken hammer.

What could I say? He'd borrowed my good hammer and never returned it, and now he'd broken my old one.

"It's my fault," he said.

I didn't argue with him. He climbed down from the stepladder and turned towards me.

"I'm going to give you my hammer," he said.

Then he reached into a brown shoe box he had in the carport and pulled out my hammer. There it was, after four years. It didn't look any different from the day he had borrowed it. I held the hammer again and it felt like a missing finger that had been reattached to my hand. So, yes, maybe he really had forgotten that it was my hammer. That didn't excuse the past four years, but at least it explained to me how a mistake could've happened.

"Go ahead, it's yours now," he said. "I owe you one, hombre."

I guess he thought I might refuse his offer to take the hammer. He looked me in the eye, and I wanted to believe that the man was telling me the truth about having forgotten. I mean, there were things I forgot now and then. Sometimes I had to look in my notebook just to remember what I was doing two days earlier. It was possible that his memory could've failed him. Anything's possible.

"Thanks, Bannert."

It felt strange to be thanking him for giving me something that was really mine, but those were the only words that came to me. I wanted to say more and set things straight with him, explain the misunderstanding, and see if maybe there was some way to put this behind us. It was just a hammer that had caused this. Maybe we could even laugh about the whole thing. I would've said something right then, but I could feel the temperature had already dropped a couple of degrees and the wind was beginning to shift. I only had a few hours left to board up my own house.

Chango

Bony was walking back from the Jiffy-Mart when he found the monkey's head. There it was, under the small palm tree in the front yard, just staring up at him like an old friend who couldn't remember his name. It freaked him out bad. The dude had to check around to make sure nobody had seen him jump back and almost drop his beer in the dirt. It was still lunchtime and cars were parked up and down the street. For a second, it looked like the head might be growing out of the ground. Maybe somebody had buried the monkey up to its neck the way people did to other people at the beach when they ran out of things to do. Maybe it was still alive. Bony grabbed a broom off the porch and swung hard. He stopped an inch away from the monkey's little black eyes, and it didn't blink. He poked the head with the straw end of the broom and it tipped back and forth. The short black hairs on its head were pointed straight up at the cloudy sky. The nose was flat and wrinkled around the edges like it'd been a normal nose and then God decided to push it in with His big thumb. The ears were old man's ears with whiskers growing on them and in them. And it kept smiling. It smiled from one monkey ear to the other.

Bony's mother said it was the ugliest thing she'd ever seen. ¡Qué feo! She wanted it out of her yard. What were the neighbors going to think? What were her customers going to say? Who would want to buy perfume from a woman who lived with such an ugly thing in her front yard? She wouldn't.

His father said it was a dead chango. He didn't care how it died or where it came from. All he knew was that Bony needed to stop lying around in his calzoncillos every morning and go out and find a job, earn some money. He was tired of coming home for lunch and seeing him sleeping on the sofa. He didn't know how a police sergeant's son could be so damn lazy. Brownsville wasn't that big a town. People talked. Bony was thirty-one years old. Ya, it was time to go do something with his life. His older brothers had good jobs. What was wrong with him? That chango wasn't going to get him anywhere. It was dead.

"I want to keep him," Bony said.

"Keep him?" his father said. "¿Estás loco o qué? You want to live with monkeys, I'll drive you to the zoo. Come on, get in the car, I'll take you right now. Marta, por favor, help your son put some clothes in a bag. He wants to live at the zoo."

"You're making your father mad, Bony."

"I didn't do anything," Bony said.

"No," his father said. "All you want to do is drink beer with your new best friend, your compadre, instead of going out to make a living."

Bony should have known his parents would say something like that. So what if he didn't have a job? Everybody had his own life.

His father drove away in the patrol car. His mother walked back inside the house. And Bony stayed in the yard with the monkey. It wasn't so bad. It's not like the head had been chopped off right there in front of the house. Except for it not having a body, the monkey was in perfect condition. The head must have come from the alley that was next to the house. People were always walking by and throwing things in the yard. It was Bony's job to keep the yard clean. His father said it was the least he could do. Every few days Bony found something new: candy wrappers, empty beer bottles, used fireworks, a dollar bill ripped in half, a fishing knife with dried blood. A few weeks earlier he'd found a busted pocket watch in the grass. Another time he found a bunch of letters from a man named Joaquín to a woman named Verónica. The letters were in Spanish, and as best as Bony could tell,

Joaquín loved Verónica and things would've worked out if he hadn't had a wife and five kids.

Most afternoons Bony sat on the tailgate of his dark blue troquita, the sound system cranked up to some Led Zeppelin or Pink Floyd. He'd been listening to the same music since high school and said he would change if another band ever came out with anything better. That afternoon was different, though. He forgot about the music and sat in a lawn chair on the grass. The shade from the fresno tree covered most of the yard. The wind was blowing some, but it was a warm breeze that made him feel like he was sitting in a Laundromat waiting for his pants to dry. He stayed cool in his chanclas, baggy blue jean shorts, and San Antonio Spurs jersey. Across the street, a crow walked in circles in front of Mando Gomez's house. Bony cracked open his first beer. The palm tree stood between him and the street. He liked being the only one who could see the monkey as people walked by that afternoon. He stared at the monkey and the monkey stared back at him.

The first ones to pass by were the chavalones walking home from school with their mommies. A few of the mommies were young and fine, but they never looked Bony's way. Next were the older kids from the junior high who lived in the neighborhood and knew better than to walk by without saying hello. "Ese Bony," they said. He pitched his head back slightly, just to let them know he'd heard them and he was cool with them.

Later, people in the neighborhood drove home from work. Some of them waved hello, some didn't. Mrs. Rivas, who lived at the other end of the street, waved only because she was friends with his mother. The old lady worked part-time in the church office and led the Rosary whenever anybody from the neighborhood died. Every Christmas, for as long as Bony could remember, she added a new animal to her Baby Jesus setting. A few years ago they sent a guy from the newspaper to take her picture surrounded by all the plastic sheep and cows in the manger. Bony did his best to avoid Mrs. Rivas, but one time she stopped her car in front of the house and invited him to a prayer group for men who were having trouble finding God. He said he wasn't having any trouble. Mrs. Rivas told him he wasn't going to find Nuestro Señor, Jesucristo, inside a can of beer. She got back in her car when Bony looked inside the can he was drinking from and said, "Hey, anybody in there?"

Domingo, the old guy who cleaned yards, usually walked by in the late afternoon and waved. Bony figured he had to be at least eighty or ninety. He'd been old like forever. Every time Bony saw Domingo he was working in people's yards and only getting older and darker. He wasn't getting rich pushing a lawn mower, that was for sure.

If it was the weekend, Ruben Ortiz might drive by. He grew up on this same street and now he was a teacher. The guy drove a nice car, wore nice clothes, even had a good-looking wife. He lived on the other side of town and came over to visit his parents. Bony could tell the guy had changed since he left the neighborhood. He'd stay in his car and wave like he was passing by in a parade. Bony thought it looked like a good life, but it wasn't for everybody, not for him anyway.

His friend Mando had big plans and look what happened

to him. He was working full-time and taking drafting classes at the college. The army paid for the classes, but he needed extra money because his girlfriend was about to have a baby. He wanted to marry her after the baby was born and buy a house, maybe a trailer to get started. Mando worked for a shuttle service that took businessmen into Matamoros. It was his job to drive them to their offices at the maquiladoras, unload any extra packages from the van, drive back across the bridge, and then pick up the same businessmen later that day. So he was driving back alone one morning, right? It was foggy on this narrow road and a truck hit him head-on. Mando died instantly, at least that's what his family hoped. Because if he didn't, it meant he was still alive when somebody stole his wallet, his gold chain with the cross, and his favorite pair of boots right off his feet. The owner of the shuttle service said the company would pay for the funeral and set aside $5,000 to give Mando's kid when he turned eighteen, but nothing more for the family. Nada más, the owner was nice enough to translate for Mando's father. The family hired a lawyer to represent them, but he was young and inexperienced and the company's lawyers weren't. Nada más ended up being all the family got. Mando's girlfriend and the baby moved in with his parents.

This thing with Mando happened a few years ago. Bony had an okay job around that time. He worked for the city, in the Parks Division, where his job was to open one of the gyms in the afternoon, hand out basketballs, break up any fights before they started, and make sure nobody stuffed anything down the toilets. He played ball if a team needed an extra player, and he had a killer jump shot from the base-line, three-point range. Nothing but net. *Swoosh!!!* Then one night he sneaks inside the gym with a girl he met at a party. She's a gordita who weighs almost twice as much as Bony, but she wants it and he has a set of gym keys that are burning a hole in his pocket. And they're having a good time, when all of a sudden the security guard pops the lights on and catches Bony and the girl rolling around at center court like they're wrestling for a loose ball. The guard is an old guy who's seri-ous about his job. He walks into the Parks Division office the next morning and reports Bony. By the end of the week, the dude's at home without a job.

Now Bony made his money installing car stereos on the side. People paid him what they could — twenty or thirty dollars was the usual — but if he knew them, he might let them slide with a case of Corona or Negra Modelo. He also helped out his mom with her Avon deliveries. She paid him a few dollars for this. At first he thought there might be some nice-looking women buying perfume, but they all turned out to be as old or older than his mom, viejitas like Mrs. Rivas. Some of the women would tip him a couple of dollars, which was better than nothing. He was getting by, and except for his parents hassling him about finding a real job, he didn't have any complaints.

It was dark when his father came home with dinner. He'd picked up a family box from Kentucky Fried Chicken. Bony liked the chicken at Church's better, liked those papitas they served, but the manager at KFC gave his dad a discount for being a police officer, and that was that. If Bony wanted Church's, he'd have to buy it with Bony's money.

His mother set the table with paper plates and napkins. Bony sat by the open blinds so he could keep an eye on the monkey. He served himself a chicken breast and some mashed potatoes. His father served himself two legs and a roll. His mother liked the wings and coleslaw. They ate without talking. The opening and closing of the red and white box was the only sound in the room. Bony's mother stood up once to find the salt. His father was scooping up the last of his mashed potatoes when he finally spoke.

"Did you know that Colonel Sanders, the man who invented Kentucky Fried Chicken, tried one hundred and twenty-four recipes before he made the perfect one? One hundred and twenty-four. What does that tell you, Bony?"

"That he should've gone to Church's."

"Why do I even try to talk sense to you?" His father shook his head and looked at Bony's mother, who stared back like she was waiting for the answer. He bit another piece off his roll, chewed it, swallowed, and spoke again.

"The Colonel, he didn't give up because he didn't get it right the first time. That's what I'm trying to say here."

"What was he a colonel of?" Bony asked.

"¿Pues, quién sabe? He was just a colonel, of the army, of the marines, of all the chickens and roosters. It doesn't matter, Bony. The point is, the man didn't give up and you shouldn't, either. You can't stay home the rest of your life because a job didn't work out. Look at the Colonel. Let him be your example."

"I'm not going to wear one of those uniforms they wear at Kentucky Fried Chicken, no way."

"Bony, all I'm saying is, there are people I can call. People who know the name Sergeant Timo Hinojosa and could help you."

"What's wrong with that?" his mother asked. "What's wrong with accepting some help from your father? That's what parents are for."

"Nothing." Bony glanced out the window.

"Don't be thinking you're going to keep that chango," his father said.

"Why not?"

"It's a dead chango," his mother said. "Do you need another reason?"

Bony walked outside and sat in the lawn chair. The porch light was on and he could see the monkey watching him. There were only three cans left in his twelve-pack. In an hour, the beer would be gone. He was about to walk to the Jiffy-Mart again, but instead he decided to hang out in the yard with the monkey. Back when Mando was around, the two of them partied all night. One time they stayed up until five in the morning, taking hits off some hash, drinking beer, and eating Doritos. Bony had heard that a volcano erupted in Mexico and was going to turn the moon a different color. And sure enough, the moon turned a dark red like there was a heart inside of it pumping blood. Mando called it the werewolf moon.

Bony stood in the middle of the street and howled as loud as he could. He howled like he'd been bitten and he was turning into a werewolf, growing fur and fangs and claws and a tail. He howled until his father opened the window and told him to shut the hell up.

Bony was sitting in the lawn chair when his father turned off the porch light. It was almost eleven o'clock. He sat in the dark staring at the monkey and barely making out the shape of its head. Usually there would've been more light in the yard, but some pendejo had busted out the streetlight again. Bony finished his last beer and closed his eyes. When he woke up a few minutes later, a cat was sniffing the monkey. "¡Pinche gato!" Bony yelled and threw a rock at it. He pegged the cat on its backside right as it was starting to lick the monkey's ear. Bony went over to make sure the monkey was all right. He cleared the dirt around the palm tree so there wouldn't be any bugs crawling on the head.

It was time to go to sleep, but he couldn't leave the monkey outside. Not if he wanted to see it again. If you left anything in the yard overnight, it was as good as gone. People chained their barbecue pits to trees. Unless you drove some cucaracha, your car better have an alarm on it. Most of the neighbors who could afford them had steel bars installed on the windows and doors of their houses, and even that didn't always keep the cabrones out if they thought there was something worth stealing. The Sanchez family had a full-grown chow in their backyard, and one day it disappeared forever. No way was he leaving the monkey in the yard.

Bony found a plastic trash bag on the porch, but he wasn't sure how to put the monkey's head inside it. He hadn't really touched the monkey, and the truth was that actually putting his hands on it was kind of freaky to him. He told himself it wasn't because he was afraid — he just didn't want to mess up its hair. If he were a monkey, he wouldn't want some guy grabbing him by the head. He wrapped his hand inside the white bag and held the head against the palm tree until he could scoop it up. When he walked into his room, Bony could see the monkey's black face pressed against the white plastic.

Where to put the monkey was the next question. There was room on the dresser if he moved his boom box, except he liked having it right under his team poster of the Dallas Cowboys. He also had a poster of the cheerleaders hanging on the back of the door, where nobody could see it and his mother wouldn't complain every time people came to the house. Two leather basketballs were sitting on the recliner he didn't use anymore. He tossed the basketballs in the closet and placed the monkey's head on the recliner. The monkey looked sharp, looked like a king sitting on his throne.

Bony turned off the lights and climbed into bed. It was pitch-black in the room except for the eyes and shiny white teeth that he swore he could see on the chair. Bony turned towards the wall, but he kept seeing the smile in his mind. He imagined what would happen if the monkey grew back its body in the middle of the night. Hairy arms and legs, long

skinny tail, sharp pointy teeth, hands that looked like feet, feet
that looked like hands. And what if this new monkey was out
for revenge against the people who had cut off its head, but
since it was a monkey, it didn't know any better and attacked
the first person it saw? It started by ripping out the person's
eyes so he couldn't fight back and then it chomped on his face
and neck, eating up his cheeks and tongue, gnawing on the
bones and cartilage, until the whole room was covered with
blood. Bony folded the pillow around his head and tried to
make himself fall asleep. After a while, he stood up and put the
monkey in the closet and pushed the chair against the door.

He woke up earlier than usual the next morning. His parents
were sitting at the kitchen table when he walked in holding
the plastic bag. The monkey was pressed against the white
plastic, staring at the chorizo con huevo on the table.

"¡Ay, Bony!" his mother said, "No me digas que you
brought that chango inside my house."

"I didn't want somebody to steal him."

"Who's going to steal a monkey head?" his father said.

"You never know."

"Take him outside, ahorita mero!" his mother said. "I will
not have a dead chango inside my house. No señor, you're
going to ruin my business."

"You heard your mother. You better get that chango out
of here."

Bony walked outside and placed the monkey back in the
same spot where it had been the day before. This time he went

ahead and held the monkey in his hands. Its fur was soft and its ears felt like human ears, kind of. His parents, as usual, were freaking out about nothing. The fur around the monkey's left ear was messed up from being inside the bag. Bony licked his palm and smoothed down the fur.

The sun was already up and it was getting warm in the neighborhood. Bony grabbed a can of Coke from the refrigerator and sat in the lawn chair. The *Herald* was lying next to the fresno tree. He opened the paper and checked out the local news, halfway expecting to see an article about somebody finding a monkey's body without a head. There was news about two Canadians getting busted at the International Bridge with heroin sealed inside cans of tuna, news about even more Border Patrol agents being hired, news about the farmers needing rain, news about the effects of the peso devaluation on downtown, news about the owner of El Chueco Bar on Fourteenth Street being attacked with a machete and surviving, but nothing about the monkey.

After he finished with the first section, he turned to the want ads. They were taking applications at the Levis plant. Parra Furniture needed a deliveryman. The security job at Amigoland Mall looked cool. All those guys did was drive around the mall and make sure your car didn't get ripped off while you were shopping. How hard could that be?

People had it wrong when they thought Bony didn't want to work. He was only trying to have a good time before it was too late. Bony used to think he and Mando would be partying for the rest of their lives. Mando had told him about school and getting married, but he never took him seriously.

Guys talked, and lots of times that's all it was, talk. It wasn't until the accident that he realized Mando had a whole different life he was planning. At first, Bony couldn't believe he was dead. It messed him up. He didn't know how to make sense of his friend dying. Bony hadn't been doing much except hanging out and partying. So why did God take Mando and not him? A couple of times he'd seen Mando's kid playing alone in the front yard and had gone over. He was a happy kid, but playing with him made Bony miss his friend, so he didn't go over that much anymore. It was better just to wave at him from this side of the street.

"¿Todavía?" Bony's father was standing on the front porch. "I thought we told you to get that chango out of here."

"I thought you meant later, or tomorrow."

"Now, Bony."

"Pues, I don't know where to take him."

"That's not my problem, Bony. That's your problem. You can drive it all the way back to Africa, or wherever it came from. I don't care." His father crossed his arms and leaned against the porch. "And I'm going to wait right here until you do it."

Bony took his time standing up and putting the monkey back in the plastic bag. He could feel his father's eyes on his back, but he didn't let it get to him. He walked down the street, trying to look like any other guy walking down the street with a monkey's head in a plastic bag. No worries. He waved to Domingo, but the old man was busy trimming the grass around a neighbor's tree. A few houses later, Bony threw a rock at the same cat from the night before.

Lincoln Park was at the end of the block. It looked more like a long, skinny island than it did a park. The palm trees were one of the few things that stood out when the resaca flooded. The water usually took a couple of weeks to go back down to its normal level, which was more than enough time for all the mosquitoes to show up.

He crossed the small bridge over the resaca. The park was empty at that hour. He climbed the wooden fort that the little kids played on during the day. This was also the fort where Mando and Bony convinced a couple of girls to come hang out with them one night. The guys were sixteen, the girls were fifteen. Bony scored two bottles of strawberry wine and they took turns going down the slide. After a while, Mando and his girl went for a long walk. Bony stayed with his girl in the fort, where she let him do everything but go inside her.

He took the monkey out of the plastic bag and set it next to him. From where he was sitting on the fort, Bony could see most of the park. If you played basketball here, you had to be a fast runner or the ball was going to be rolling into the water every game. This was the court where Bony first got his shot down. Next to the basket were the picnic tables that filled up fast on the weekends. You could forget barbecuing here unless you started setting up way before noon. If they were having a lowrider show in the park, you'd be lucky to find a place to sit.

By the water fountains was where Bony had stopped a guy named Javier Ortiz. The girl Mando had been with that night in the park was Javier's old girlfriend, and now Javier was saying he was going to jump Mando.

"I heard you were talking shit about Mando."

"What's it to you?"

"You got a problem with Mando, you got a problem with me."

"No, man, I don't have no problems with you," Javier said. "It's cool."

"I think you do, puto. And I think I'm going to kick your ass," Bony said.

And then he did.

Bony looked down and saw that flies were buzzing around the monkey's head and landing on its nose. He shooed them away with his hand, but they kept coming back. Looking at the long whiskers on the monkey's cheeks, the deep lines around its eyes, made him want to find out where the head had come from. Bony thought about calling the zoo and asking them if they were missing any monkeys, but then he figured that if a monkey had been kidnapped, they might be tracing the phone calls and he'd get blamed for the whole thing. He didn't need that kind of trouble.

He walked back to the house remembering all the monkeys he'd seen on TV or at the movies, but none of them looked like his monkey. He thought how weird it was that he'd never seen one like this before. When he made it home, he put the monkey in the truck and drove out of the neighborhood. He passed the park and headed down International, in the direction of the library. Pink Floyd was on the stereo and the woofers were maxed out enough for people to feel the vibrations two cars over. The monkey was riding shotgun.

The library parking lot was full, so Bony had to circle around a few times to find a spot. He left the monkey on the floor mat, where people couldn't see it. As soon as he felt how cold it was inside the library, he wished he'd worn long pants. The encyclopedias were on a short bookcase close to the entrance. He sat in a chair and read about the differences between monkeys and apes. The most interesting part was how much they were related to humans. He'd never been completely comfortable with that idea, but at the same time he didn't know what to make of the story of Adam and Eve and a talking snake. Even if he did believe people came from monkeys, he had to ask where the monkeys came from.

The encyclopedia had a life-size picture of a gorilla's hand. Bony placed his own hand on top of the gorilla's hand, and although his was a lot smaller, they did match. The encyclopedia had pictures of more monkeys and apes than he ever knew existed, but he couldn't find a picture that looked exactly like his monkey's head. He finally spotted one in a book called *Monkeys of the New World*. In the picture, the black monkey was standing on a tree branch picking fruit. It was a spider monkey, from Ecuador. Bony read about what they ate, how long they lived, how they took care of their babies. He even checked out a picture of two spider monkeys having sex, which he didn't look at for too long because he didn't want the library lady walking by and thinking he was some weirdo.

He put the monkey back on the passenger seat as he drove home. Now that Bony had learned something about the monkey, he wanted to name it. The first thing that popped into his mind was to call it Spider Man because he kind of liked the guy in the comics. He thought about naming it Blackie, but he knew that was dumb. Zorro was kind of a cool name, but there was already a black dog on his street named Zorro. He couldn't remember Tarzan's monkey's name, or that might have worked. Then he tried to think of a name in Spanish, but the only name he came up with was the easiest, Chango. He hadn't liked it when his parents used the word because they only used it to say it was a dead chango. But the more he thought about it, it fit. He liked the way it sounded when he said it to himself: Chango, Chango, Chango. Ese Chango. Bony and Chango.

Bony stopped at the Jiffy-Mart and bought a twelve-pack. It was three o'clock by the time he stopped in front of the house. His mother and Mrs. Rivas were standing next to the palm tree. Mrs. Rivas held a small plastic bottle upside down and squirted water on the ground. Bony placed Chango on the floor mat and grabbed the beer as he stepped out of the truck.

"Agua bendita," Mrs. Rivas said as he walked up.

He stepped back when he realized it really was holy water.

"¿Dónde está el chango, Bony?" she asked.

"What chango?"

"I already told Mrs. Rivas what you found," his mother said. "She says somebody's trying to put a curse on our house, maybe on my business."

"No they're not, it's just a monkey's head. What's the big deal?"

"¿Qué crees, Bony?" Mrs. Rivas said. "Eh, you think God opened the heavens and dropped that chango's head in your yard so you could tell him your jokes? No, mi'jo, that's the work of brujas."

"That's crazy. There's no brujas."

"Listen to her, Bony." His mother held his arm.

"You think brujas are like you see them on the television, flying around on brooms, but that's not the way it is. You don't know. ¿Tú qué sabes? They shop at the mall, eat at Luby's, go to bailes and dance cumbias. Brujas are everywhere, Bony, probably in this neighborhood."

The old lady looked down the street and then back at Bony.

"Go ask Mrs. Molina, on the next block. Ask her what happened to her mother. Andale, she'll tell you how somebody threw a dead snake in her mother's yard, y la pobre mujer, she stepped on it barefoot. The very next morning her skin started falling off. I wouldn't lie to you, Bony, *her skin.* Until there was nothing left of the woman. Tell me that's not the work of brujas."

"¿Ya ves? You're bringing curses into my house."

"Now tell us where you put that chango's head," Mrs. Rivas said.

"We already checked in your room, mi'jo," his mother said.

"You what?"

"Your mother was worried about the curses."

"He wasn't hurting anybody."

"Tell us where it is, Bony," Mrs. Rivas said.

"I threw him away already."

"Where, Bony?" his mother said.

"In the trash, behind the Jiffy-Mart."

"Are you telling your mother the truth, Bony?" Mrs. Rivas said.

"Go see for yourself if you don't believe me."

Mrs. Rivas and his mother looked at each other. Bony walked to the porch and leaned back in the lawn chair. It was just another afternoon in the neighborhood. After a few minutes Mrs. Rivas drove away.

"Más vale que me estés diciendo la verdad, Bony," his mother said. "I better not see that monkey in my house again."

Bony shook his head. "Don't worry."

She walked into the house and let the screen door slam shut.

Bony stayed on the porch. Across the street, Mando's kid was riding his tricycle through the front yard. It was quiet in the neighborhood. Bony cracked open his first beer. The can was sweating in his hand and down onto the porch. He took a drink and kicked back. He wasn't going to let anybody take Chango.

Except for walking inside to grab a piece of leftover chicken, Bony sat on the porch for the rest of the afternoon. He thought his mother might be watching him through the window and he didn't want to make her suspicious. The beer was cold. What more did he need, right?

His parents ate dinner at seven, but Bony stayed outside on the porch. He went in later and microwaved what was left of the tacos they'd had for dinner. His father was in the kitchen cleaning his work shoes. The patent leather was shiny and Bony kept looking at his own reflection.

"You drink too much," his father said.

"So what?"

"*So what?* This isn't a cantina, where you can get pedo and stare at somebody's shoes. What's wrong with you?"

Bony didn't answer and took another bite of his taco.

"Your mother says you're sad because we made you throw away the chango."

"I'm not sad."

"You look sad."

"I'm just thinking."

"Are you thinking about what kind of job you're going to look for tomorrow?"

"Not really."

"I didn't think so."

After Bony was done eating, he drank another beer and watched a baseball game on TV. He hated baseball, but he was waiting for his parents to go to sleep, which they finally did a little after ten. He grabbed Chango from the truck and put him under the small palm tree. The moon was almost full and its glow filled the yard with light. Bony brought out his lawn chair, just like old times. There was half a can of beer left, which he placed next to Chango. He could see himself doing this every night. His parents never had to find out. Maybe one of these nights when they were away from the house, he and Chango would cook out in the backyard. Some fajitas, some chicken, some beer. It'd be badass. People would be walking by and going, "¿Qué onda, Bony?" And he'd be like, "Aquí nomás. Just cooking out, man." And they'd walk away thinking the dude knew how to do it right.

It was after midnight when Bony put away the lawn chair and carried Chango back to the truck. He didn't want to risk taking him inside the house and his parents finding out. Earlier he'd left a crack at the top of the windows, but now he rolled them up in case there was rain. He locked the truck and went inside the house.

He tried to relax in bed and enjoy what was left of his beer buzz. Tomorrow he'd figure out what to do with Chango. Maybe his mother would forget about what Mrs. Rivas had said. His father might be okay with him keeping Chango if he went out and found a job. Bony thought anything could happen. He might even fall asleep and turn into a monkey overnight, and then his parents would have to keep him and Chango.

It felt like he'd only been asleep for five minutes when he heard a fire engine driving through the front yard. He sat up in bed and realized it was already morning and the siren was really the alarm on his truck. His father was standing next to the truck with his hands cupped over his ears. Bony's mother walked towards the house when he opened the front door. He deactivated the alarm and then locked the truck again before his father could open the door.

"¡Ya lo vi, Bony!" his mother said. "I knew you were lying. ¡Güerco embustero! ¡Ahora verás!"

"What? He's not even close to the house."

"Bony, you knew what I meant."

"Ya fue mucho," his father said. "I'm going to call the city to come pick up the chango and take it away." He walked inside the house and grabbed the phone.

"I'll keep him somewhere else," Bony said.

His father shook his head and opened the phone book.

"What if I get a job?"

"It's too late, Bony." His father dialed a number.

Bony finished getting dressed and went to his truck. He drove out of the neighborhood, not sure where he was going exactly. Chango sat in the passenger seat, smiling as usual. Bony rolled down the windows and listened to the wind. There wasn't that much traffic on International that early in the morning. He drove past Southmost Road and slowed down for the flashing yellow light in front of la Porter, his old high school, so he wouldn't get pulled over by a cop. When he was on the other side of Four Corners, he stopped at a convenience store. A carton of orange juice and a package of cinnamon rolls were what he needed right now. Jumping out of bed so fast had made him feel extra crudo.

The orange juice came with little chunks of ice, the way he liked it, but he had to be careful not to get the steering wheel sticky while he was driving and eating the cinnamon rolls. It felt like a road trip is what it felt like. They could drive anywhere they wanted to, Corpus, San Antonio, Houston, anywhere. He and Mando had always talked about someday taking a trip to see the Dallas Cowboys play. If he had more than two dollars in his pocket, he might have taken off right then. Instead, he turned down 511 and drove around the edge of town. There were a couple of new subdivisions, but it was still mainly farmland out there. Back in high school, Bony used to like to party and then go cruising. He remembered driving on this road alone one night and almost hitting a cow that was standing in the middle of the road. It came out of nowhere. He blinked and there it was, staring into the headlights. Bony had to swerve to miss it and then swerve back onto the road so he wouldn't hit a telephone pole. It could've easily been his time to go, but it wasn't. And now here he was with Chango.

He drove around for the rest of the morning and tried to come up with a plan. They traveled down Paredes, Coffeeport Road, Fourteenth Street, 802, Central, and Boca Chica. Going everywhere and nowhere at the same time. People were in a hurry to get places, but Bony and Chango were taking their time. On Palm Boulevard, they passed the big, expensive houses with trimmed lawns and then turned left at the first light. They drove another block and stopped in a parking lot across the street from the zoo.

Bony turned off the engine and listened for the animal sounds. He had to wait for a couple of school buses to turn the corner before it was quiet. All he could hear were the birds on the phone lines and a dog barking in the distance. He hadn't been to the zoo in years, but he was almost sure the monkeys were on a little island on the other side of the tall fence. Bony tried to imagine how he would've escaped if he were a monkey. Chango probably had it planned out months ahead of time, knew when the zoo people left at night, knew the perfect time to make a break for it. Chango was looking for something more than what he was going to find on that little island. Nobody could blame him for that.

Fifteen minutes went by before Bony started up the truck again. He was pulling out of the parking lot when he heard the monkey calls from the other side of the street. He looked at Chango, but Chango kept looking straight ahead.

They drove back to the neighborhood. Bony passed by his street and saw a city truck parked in front of the house. He drove on until he was on the other side of Lincoln Park. Two old men were sitting in a station wagon by the entrance. They were drinking beer and listening to a ranchera station. Bony parked a few spaces away from their car. He put Chango inside the plastic bag. The old men were laughing hard like one of the men had told the other a funny joke. They happened to look up at Bony as he was getting out of the truck, and the man in the driver's seat nodded hello to him. Bony nodded back to him and walked into the park with Chango.

He crossed a short bridge and stepped down to the canal. He took Chango out of the bag and sat by the edge of the water. The resaca that surrounded the park ended up here and then dropped off a small concrete waterfall. Bony and Mando had learned to fish in this canal. They used a couple of branches, some fishing line, hooks, and bread that Bony had taken from his mother's kitchen. Beginner's luck, that's what Mando called it when Bony caught a shiner that first afternoon. He called it luck whenever Bony beat him at something. In a lot of ways, he was lucky that he'd found Chango. How many guys could say they'd found a monkey's head in their front yard? He'd probably never find anything like this again. He was sure that if Chango were a guy they'd be camaradas. Same thing would go if Bony were a monkey. They'd be hanging out in the jungle, swinging from trees, eating bananas. They'd be putting the moves on all the changuitas, doing it monkey-style. He would miss his truck, but then what would he need it for in the jungle? It's not like there was anywhere to go cruising. And if he were a monkey, nobody would be hassling him to be something else. He'd be a monkey. He wouldn't have to go to school, or work, or file for unemployment. And something else: monkeys were always together. He and Chango would be friends until they were viejitos, all wrinkled and hunched over and walking from tree to tree because they were too old to be swinging. They'd be hanging out forever. "Right?" Bony said. "Right?" It took a second before he realized that he was talking to himself.

The water was browner and greener than he remembered it. A tire had washed up on the other side of the canal. An army boot floated and got stuck on some lily pads. He broke a dead branch into four pieces and pitched them into the water one at a time. When he ran out of branches and twigs, he threw pebbles. Time was passing slowly and he was avoiding doing what he had to do. Bony skipped a few more rocks across the water. He wished people would leave him alone, let him live his own life. If he drank, it was because he wanted to drink. If he stayed at home without a real job, it was because he wasn't ready for that yet. There wasn't anybody who understood him. He and Chango were hanging out. His mother and father didn't know what they were saying. His mother let herself be talked into crazy ideas by Mrs. Rivas. People were always talking at him and telling him how he should live. Sometimes he listened, but most times he didn't. He was just living. That's the best explanation he could give. Living. Bony leaned over and held Chango a couple of inches above the water. It was the last thing in the world that he wanted to do, but he let go.

They Say He Was Lost

Domingo

This morning after the storm, the edge of the alley was the only dry place a man could wait for a ride. Water filled the gutter and spilled over into large puddles. A toad had been squashed in the middle of the street; its guts trailed down toward the curb. Tree branches leaned against power lines. Domingo squatted on his haunches, far enough away from the smell of wet trash and a dead tacuache that lay stiff in the middle of the alley. He tilted back his straw cowboy hat. His machete hung off the side of his belt. He had been waiting over half an hour for la señora Ross. If she did not come soon, he would have to start working after the sun had already made the day hot. He was not afraid of hard work, but at seventy-three years of age he knew it was important to work slowly and be sure the job was done well. As he waited for la señora, he tried to distract himself with different thoughts of how his day would go, but his mind drifted back to the same thought he had woken up with that morning: today was the birthday of his Sara. She would have been twenty-one years old on this day, a woman with her own family by now. He knew his wife was back home doing something to remember their daughter, to remember the one year she was with them. Like so many times before, Domingo tried to imagine what Sara might look like as a grown woman, but he saw her only as a little girl and this brought back some old feelings he had worked hard to silence. He was thankful when he saw that la señora had finally arrived.

Domingo opened the car door and la señora's little dog barked and barked. The dog had long brown hair and little black eyes that seemed to pop out of its head.

"Bueno días," la señora said.

"Buenos días, señora," Domingo said.

"Mucho trabajo at la casa," she said.

These were the same words they said every Saturday morning when she arrived for him. La señora spoke very little Spanish and Domingo even less English. They had learned to communicate with their own sign language, which was made up of the physical motions of what they were trying to say. There was a sign for Domingo to sweep the grass off the sidewalk and driveway. A sign told him exactly how to trim the bushes. Another sign let la señora know that the lawn mower needed more gasoline. The sign they used the most was the one to say that it was very hot. La señora would wipe her brow with the back of her hand. "Mucho calor," Domingo would say. "Mucho, mucho calor," la señora said. "Sí, hace mucho calor," Domingo said. If there was something they couldn't figure out a sign for, la señora would go next door and ask for help from the girl who cleaned her neighbor's house.

This Saturday, la señora stopped on the way to her house. She motioned for Domingo to wait in the car. She left the air conditioner on the HIGH setting and turned the radio dial to a Tejano station, smiling as she did this. He understood that she had adjusted the radio for him, but he had never cared for that type of music and the disturbing sound created with so many instruments. In any case, it was difficult to hear any-thing because the little dog would not stop barking. Where he came from, someone would have beaten the dog by now. Domingo tried to ignore the animal and enjoy the cold air. He put his face up to the vent and felt the air blow through his eyebrows.

When they finally arrived at the house, la señora showed him the area of the backyard where several branches had bro-ken off the ebony tree and fallen over the patio area. Two smaller branches were floating in the light blue water of the swimming pool. He used his machete to cut the pieces so he could stuff them into the plastic trash cans. Later, la señora asked him to use a long pole with a net at the end to scoop out the tiny leaves in the pool. Domingo liked working for her because he knew he was guaranteed work for the entire day. Her property was much larger than those in the neighborhood where he usually worked. She also owned a new lawn mower that was more powerful than any he had ever used. La señora was very particular about her yard and how she wanted it maintained. The grass along the sidewalk needed to be trimmed a certain way so that it met up with the pavement but did not hang over the edge. Domingo took pride in his work and wanted la señora to be pleased with the way her yard looked.

At lunchtime, la señora's daughter brought out two ham and cheese sandwiches for him to eat. The young lady had a pleasant smile, and it was hard for him not to wonder how beautiful his own daughter might have been, but he knew these feelings would not do him any good and he tried his best to distract himself with other thoughts. He was hungry by this hour of the day, so he ate everything she brought out to him. He sat in a lawn chair under the patio umbrella, imagining this was how people of money ate when they stayed in hotels. The sandwiches were filling, but at his age the spicy mustard upset his stomach. He would have mentioned this to la señora, except he didn't have the words to say it, and even if he did, he didn't want to seem unappreciative.

He was finishing his lunch when la señora came out to show him what she wanted him to do next. She made a hacking sign to tell Domingo that he needed to cut some more broken branches left from last night's storm. The tallest limbs were cracked and hanging on to the house. He nodded and made a motion as if he were climbing a tall ladder. La señora walked with him to the garage, where she kept the larger tools.

Domingo gazed up at the sky as he climbed the aluminum ladder, stepping lightly on each rung. The white clouds floating over the Rio Grande Valley appeared close enough for a man to reach out and touch with his hand. Sweat was streaming down his face, and the band of his hat was drenched. His machete hung off the back of his belt. The ladder wobbled slightly as he hacked at broken branches, and he thought he might have been more secure on the rungs if he had climbed barefoot. He would have done this, but he was embarrassed to show his tired, cracked feet in front of la señora. They were the feet of an old man who had worked his whole life like a mule. Some of the jobs he took paid very little, but he felt fortunate to still be working. No one could say he had ever backed down from a day's work.

He had to climb onto the roof to reach some branches that were near the antenna. Domingo looked down and saw la señora watching him. The roof was over thirty feet high, and it occurred to him that this was the highest place he had ever worked. La señora owned a two-story house that was bigger than most of the houses on her street. From where he was perched, he could see the red arch on the Matamoros side of the bridge. If he stood on his toes, he could barely make out the tops of the billboards that invited tourists to drink more rum and eat dinner at restaurants across the river.

Seeing this little bit of his country made him think of his home. It also made him think of Sara.

La señora was yelling something up to him, but he couldn't understand what she was trying to say.

"¿Mande, señora?"

She jerked her hands up as if she were being shocked, and Domingo understood he wasn't supposed to touch the antenna. He waved back to let her know that he understood.

One by one, he cut the branches loose and let them fall to the ground, making sure they landed a good distance from where la señora was standing. As he worked, his memory took him back home. He could see the baby walking the way she did, like a little drunk man. She crawled faster than this, but she was determined to walk on her own. Sara was always learning new things, which made Domingo and his wife believe God had blessed them with an intelligent child. He thought now that if he had stopped her from trying to walk and made her crawl, maybe she would not have been so curious to see what was down in the pit. His wife had asked him to build a fire so she could heat water to wash clothes. He turned around for a second. Even now he had trouble understanding why his wife had left him with the baby. They took her to a woman who knew how to heal, but she offered them only prayers. They borrowed money from their family to take her to a clinic, but there they told them her brain had been damaged by the fire in the pit and the best they could do was keep her comfortable. They asked God for a miracle. The women of the family prayed a Rosary over the little girl every day.

Domingo and his wife made a promesa that if their baby were to get better, they would walk the ten or twelve days it took them to get from where they lived outside of Ciudad Mante to Mexico City, in order to visit the Basilica, and, on their knees, give thanks to the Virgen de Guadalupe. And still the child suffered for a month until the night she died. After they buried her, Domingo told himself he would never enter another church unless he was carried through the doors in a wooden box. But he knew this was wrong, and for a long time he had wanted to make peace with these bitter feelings. As he looked toward the river, he thought that today, on Sara's birthday, might be a good time to speak to God. He wished he could go back and be with his wife, cross the bridge and buy a ticket for the next bus headed south. But he had to remind himself that he had been home less than a month earlier and getting back across was becoming more difficult with the immigration authorities stationed along the river. He concentrated on the work he was doing, letting the machete fall harder on the broken branches, but the need to find peace in his heart would not leave him.

The sun was lowering itself by the time Domingo returned to the little room where he slept. The room belonged to the Ramirez brothers and was attached to their tire shop. They allowed him to stay there for free, with the understanding that he would watch over the repair shop at night. Since the brothers also stored tires in the room, the space for his cot was limited. He was grateful to them for offering him a place to sleep, but he never stayed in bed too long, because of the loneliness it brought him and the fact that the smell of so much rubber gave him a headache. His clothes were stored in a cardboard box under the cot. The only other belongings he placed inside the box were a photo of his wife with the baby and a tattered envelope with the directions for where to send his money back home.

After he washed his hands and face at the sink inside the garage, he put on a pair of jeans and a green shirt la señora had given him. The jeans fit a little big in the waist, but that was what belts were for. He used a rag to clean the dust off his black shoes until they looked presentable. Then he grabbed his hat and locked up the little room.

Holy Family Church was a short walk from where Domingo lived. He had passed by the church many times but had never considered attending the Spanish mass they offered Saturday evenings. By this hour, the services had ended and he was hoping to have a moment alone before the altar. He had always considered the church small compared with most churches he knew in Mexico, but now as he walked toward the entrance, he felt as if he were approaching a very large mountain. The saints on the stained-glass windows looked like images he had seen once in a long, fitful dream. Domingo pulled on the large wooden doors, but they were locked. He peered through the window and saw a single light shining down on the altar. He walked around to the side of the building, but the doors were locked there as well. In all his years, he had never seen a church with its doors locked. Perhaps his imagination, or even God himself, was playing tricks on him for having stayed away so long. But the doors were just as locked the second time he tried.

Domingo was heading back to his room when he saw a couple, an older man and woman, walking with a small gray and white dog. The man used a cane and looked at least ten years older than Domingo. The woman was younger than her husband and she held the dog's leash. Domingo greeted the couple and asked them if they knew why the church doors were locked. The old man said he truthfully did not know the answer to this question, but perhaps it had something to do with the priest not wanting to work late. The man's wife shook her head and said the real reason was that the church had been broken in to too many times, and once, it had even caught on fire accidentally. She doubted whether he would find any church in town open at this hour. Domingo thanked them and kept walking.

When he arrived back at his room, he lay on the cot and rested. Sometimes he bought beer and drank outside the room on a wooden stool. But he tried not to do that anymore, because it was difficult for him to stop after two or three beers and then he would miss work because he overslept. All he wanted now was to fall asleep and forget his failed trip to the church. The room was dark except for a ray of light that leaked in through a corner of the ceiling. He wondered if there was some way of entering another church, at least to light a candle and say a short prayer. So much time had passed, and now waiting another night felt like an eternity, the same eternity he and his wife had endured while they waited for God to bless them with a child. For years, he had felt cursed because his woman had not become pregnant. She was younger and healthier than he was. There was no reason for them not to share in this blessing. And finally, when they had lost all hope of bringing a child into the world, Sara was born. How then could the child have been taken from them so quickly? Domingo blamed himself for not having kept her away from the pit. He carried the guilt on his back as if it were a load of firewood that was added to with each passing year. It was impossible for him to make sense of the tragedy. How could God have permitted it to happen? And then Domingo remembered something he had seen not so long ago. He was riding in la señora's car when they drove by a house where people were standing on the street praying. Someone had discovered the image of the Virgin Mary in the trunk of an álamo tree. The shape of the Virgin Mother's face and arms were formed into the bark. People were staring up at the image from both sides of the street, and the group closest to the tree was praying a Rosary. A slender woman with short hair was pushing a young boy in a wheelchair. The boy's spine was arched as if he were trying to reach a knife stuck in his back. He wore a large bib and his head was swollen to the size of a pumpkin. Next to the tree, an older woman with a long braid knelt at an altar. A man leaned against a fence with his one leg, while his right pant leg, folded in half and sewn up underneath him, flapped in the wind like a small brown flag. Domingo remembered that la señora honked her car horn at a woman standing in the middle of the street with her head bowed and her arms reaching toward the Virgin Mary. He didn't understand what la señora had said, but he knew it had something to do with all the people in the street.

Domingo put on his clothes and locked the door to his room again. As much as he wanted to do something to remember Sara's birthday, he could not escape the question of whether the image was truly the Virgin, though he reasoned that so many people could not be wrong. After all, they were people who possessed much more faith than he had in the past twenty years. What right did he have to question their beliefs?

The road leading to the bridge was backed up with cars for several blocks. There seemed to be as many headlights as there were flashing lights announcing the rate of the peso at the various money-exchange houses. Domingo could see young people laughing and having a good time as they waited in traffic. There was one car full of young women and they all waved at Domingo as if they knew him. The light turned green and he crossed the busy street near the college and the McDonald's restaurant. He loved the hamburgers they served and eating lunch there on Sunday, his day off, was one of the few pleasures he allowed himself. He had to admit that the Americans made very good hamburgers, which was another reason to admire how advanced this country was.

He was a block away from the center of town when he saw the cathedral. Before he could check to see if the doors were open, he noticed that the steel gates were locked. The lights in the courtyard were on and he stopped to look up at

the towers stretching into the night sky. He imagined that if a
man could stand on top of one of these towers he might be
able to reach heaven, maybe even see an angel.

Half a block from the cathedral, someone whistled out to
him. Two women were standing near the entrance of El Econó-
mico Hotel. The taller one had broad shoulders and wore a
sequined tube top with a tight miniskirt. Her companion had
long blond hair that stood out against her dark skin.

"Venga pa'ca, papacito."

"¿Por qué andas con tanta prisa?"

Domingo might have stopped if he were a younger man
and it were a different night, but only until he realized they
were actually men dressed as women. The shorter one called
out to him to slow down, that they didn't bite, not very hard
anyway. Domingo looked at the different storefronts as he
walked away. One store had piles and piles of used clothing
covering the floor like giant anthills. At the next corner, he
heard norteño music coming from down the street. Men and
women were laughing and stumbling out of a cantina. He
had never entered these places near the center of town, thinking that no one wanted to see an old man drinking and feeling sorry for himself.

The bus station was a plain white building that would
have gone unnoticed by most people if it were not for the
buses heading to the North every hour. Taxis were lined up in
front of the terminal, waiting for the passengers that had arrived. The station faced the levee and the International Bridge.
Domingo recognized the sounds of the nightlife coming from

across the river, but he continued to walk as though he had not heard anything.

He turned the corner in front of the station and walked two blocks before he saw the tree. A man was kneeling at the altar. His wife stood trembling next to him, one hand on her husband's shoulder and the other hand on an aluminum walker. As the husband prayed beneath the tree, Domingo could see the image of the Virgin Mary with her arms wide open.

Now that he was finally looking at the tree up close, he didn't know if he could pray beneath it, if he could see it as more than just a tree. He wanted to believe this was the work of God. It was God who had made the tree, so He must have also created the image of the Virgin Mary. Domingo remembered the famous story of Juan Diego and how the image of the Virgen de Guadalupe appeared before him in the hills of Tepeyac and how at first nobody believed him. Domingo wondered how one man could have so much faith in his beliefs. He felt a deep sorrow for having turned his back on God because of the misfortunes in his life.

When the man finished praying at the altar, he wiped away his tears and helped his wife into their car. Saliva ran off her chin and onto her T-shirt. The husband placed the walker inside the trunk and drove away.

Domingo removed his hat and made the sign of the cross as he knelt at the altar. A chain-link fence stood between him and the image. Next to the tree was a white house with its lights off. As much as he wanted to make peace with God, he felt strange kneeling beneath the tree. The truth was, he wanted to leave and wait until the morning when the churches would open, but he couldn't allow this day to pass him by. People had left dozens of photos tacked onto a large piece of plywood leaning against the fence. He looked at the pictures — three men standing next to an elderly woman sitting in a rocking chair, a young soldier back from the war, an older woman wearing a graduation gown, a wrecked car, a retarded woman sitting next to a giant teddy bear, a newborn baby with tubes connected to his mouth and belly — and tried to set aside his doubts. Domingo bowed his head and prayed to the Virgin Mary to please send a message to his Sara. He wanted her to know that her father had kept her memory alive and that he always would as long as God gave him air to breathe. He had not forgotten what day this was, and if she were here, he himself would sing "Las Mañanitas" to her, the same way her mother had done on her first birthday. He explained to the Virgin how much he wanted to be on a bus headed home so he could wake up the next morning to the warm touch of his wife. He missed her cooking and being able to share his meals with her. Then he remembered that the reason he had come to the tree was to ask for God's forgiveness. Domingo felt ashamed for having put his desires first. He begged the Virgin to help him ask for mercy. He and his wife had lost their little girl, and he, who had always believed in the hand of God, had turned away when his prayers went unanswered. He pleaded with the Virgin to intervene on his behalf and ask God for another chance to show his devotion and become His most faithful servant once again. He had tried to be a good man all the years God had given him on earth. He had worked hard to provide for his family. Everyone knew this about him. He swore he would have been a good father to Sara if there had been more time. Then he tried to pray an avemaría, except it had been so long since he had prayed that he could not remember more than the first verse. There was a tightness in his chest and he was having trouble breathing. He tried hard to remember another prayer. Domingo begged the Virgin to forgive him, but now he felt as though he were speaking to himself: he was lost beneath the tree.

He stepped back from the altar. The people in the photos seemed to be laughing at him, as if it had been a trick all along. He felt foolish for having believed that he could find the Virgin Mother in the bark of a tree, that he could ask for God's forgiveness by kneeling at an altar on a city street. The tree had no special powers except the ones people placed on it. He was not going to find peace with God here, not any more than he was going find it on la señora's roof or in the little room where he slept every night. Domingo turned his back to the tree and walked away.

People were boarding the same bus that had arrived earlier. He could see a young couple with their arms around each other. The young woman was crying as the man boarded the bus. A mother walked on board holding her little girl by the hand. An older woman wearing a baseball cap carried two large plastic bags filled with grapefruits. A man in short pants held a large radio. The bus driver took each of their tickets. Domingo hesitated on the street corner, asking himself what he should do next. The music was louder from the other side of the river now. All he had to do was walk up the small grassy embankment to see the lights of his country. The thought of going down to the edge of the river entered his mind, but he remembered how dangerous it could be if the authorities spotted him. The bus stopped next to him and waited for the traffic light to turn green. When Domingo looked up, the little girl was looking out the window. Her mother held her in the seat and the little girl stared at Domingo. There was nothing unusual about them, but seeing them pull away, he felt they could've been his own wife and daughter if his life had turned out differently, or if only he would've had more faith. He watched the bus disappear into the center of town, and he walked back to the tree.

Domingo passed the altar and climbed onto the fence. Then he pulled himself up to the first limb. He stood and gently tossed his shoes into the grass, careful not to wake the people who lived in the house next to the tree. The second branch was more difficult, but he strained and pulled until he was standing on it. He slid his feet along so he could get to the final branch. To reach it, he stood on his toes and then swung his right leg over the top. He was thankful that his body did not fail him. He held on to the tree. This last branch was higher than la señora's roof. He could see most of the city and the few cars that were on the street. The wind was strong and he held his hat in one hand. He closed his eyes as the wind blew through his hair. He prayed again, but this time he prayed to God directly. He told God that he was a poor man who had tried to comprehend the mysteries of life. Perhaps this was something no man could comprehend, but in his heart he needed to know why he and his wife had lost their child. And now almost twenty years later, he had discovered there was no answer: it had been the will of God. There was nothing he could do but accept the life he had been given. He asked God for forgiveness and then, for just a second, he let go of the tree in order to make the sign of the cross. In that moment, he felt light enough to blow away like a leaf. It frightened him at first, but he forced himself to let go of the tree again. This time he kept his arms open and waited for his fear to pass. When he opened his eyes, he gazed out toward the horizon, farther than he had ever imagined he could. He looked across the river, past the nightclub lights on Obregón, past the shoeshine stands in Plaza Hidalgo, past the bus station where he caught his long ride home, past all the little towns and ranchitos on the way to Ciudad Victoria, past the Sierra Madre and the endless shrines for people who had died along the road, and even farther, past the loneliness of his little room next to the tire shop, past the reality that he would work the rest of his life and still die poor, and finally, past the years of sorrow he had spent remembering his little girl, past all this, until he clearly saw his wife and then his daughter, Sara, who was now a grown woman.

Big Jesse, Little Jesse

J esse lives in a small apartment three miles from the house where he used to live with his wife and son. Even now, a year after moving out, he still wonders how he went from being just another guy in the neighborhood to being married with a kid — getting up in the middle of the night, changing stinky diapers, wiping stinky butts, figuring out baby car seats, paying doctor's bills, watching cartoon videos, teaching the boy how to ride a bike, teaching him how not to fall on his face — to being separated, which is a nice way of saying "almost divorced," all before he turned twenty-four. Jesse

and Corina's reasons for not being together are more compli-
cated than there being another woman or another guy, or their
love having faded. The problems have to do with their kid.
The boy turned out like his mother, so it's no mystery to Jesse
why he likes her more. Little Jesse has her features, same light
brown hair, same dark eyes, same light skin that sometimes
makes people think they're Anglo. He's also smart like his
mother. He was reading before he started kindergarten. You
can't drag him out of the library. That's all he does, read
books, so at least he's good at it. They have a park down the
street, but you'll never see him there. He has no interest in
playing outside or watching Jesse show him his famous
around-the-back reverse layup. Jesse tried to get him to make
friends with the other boys in the neighborhood, except he
was always too shy. Then a couple of them picked on him,
called him names, and he came home crying. Jesse's wife
wouldn't let Jesse walk over and say anything to the little
punks. And she especially didn't want Jesse pushing him to
go outside anymore. She'd rather Little Jesse keep his nose
glued to the inside of a book. She wants him to get good
grades and go to college someday. There's that, and the fact
the kid was born with a physical disability. To Jesse, what he
has is one leg shorter than the other. The difference is only an
inch or so, but he used to limp enough to remind Jesse of one
those indios begging for spare change on the bridge from
Matamoros. That was before the boy started wearing a special shoe on his left foot. The shoe looks any other shoe until
you get up close and see the giant sole that makes you think it

has to be a defect from the factory. Nobody would want his boy or girl born this way, but Jesse tells himself it's not the end of the world. He's known lots of people who had something wrong with them and they didn't sit around the house all day, reading. He remembers there used to be a blind mechanic who lived in the neighborhood when he was growing up. Corina always listens to Jesse's stories, but afterward he never feels that she's made the connection between Little Jesse's disability and the "disability" in the story. Anyway, this mechanic's name was Pano, and according to Jesse, the man was blind enough to have a dog lead him around if he wanted to. His eyes moved back and forth and all around like a pair of marbles on the dashboard of a car. People said he'd gone blind at forty-six because he kept drinking his cervecitas and never took care of his diabetes. He received disability checks for a year or two, until he couldn't stand being inside the house and opened his own garage. People weren't rushing out to have a blind man fix their cars. But with time, word spread that he charged half as much as most garages and guaranteed his work. Pano had customers waiting for him to open up every morning. He did it all by the sound of the engine. Sure, he had some young guys working for him, doing the heavy work, sometimes describing what the engine and hoses looked like, but in the end, it was Pano who could find what was wrong with your car better than a garage full of mechanics with good eyes. Some people claimed that he was a better mechanic since he'd gone blind. So, no, Jesse doesn't feel sorry for his boy. He won't let himself. Little Jesse can see, hear, speak. He's smart. He's a good-looking boy. And, really, if his mother ever let him, he'd grow up normal like every other kid.

It's Sunday and Jesse drives to the house. Yesterday he called and told Corina that he wanted to barbecue. Usually he waits for some special occasion to cook out, but this time it's only that he's tired of being in the apartment alone. Corina and Little Jesse aren't back from church when he parks in front of the house. He still has a key, but he feels weird being inside when Corina isn't there. After a few minutes of sitting in the car, he walks around to the back and sets the coals in the barbecue pit, starts the fire. He sits on the back steps and watches the flames flicker over the top of the pit. The yard looks nice, maybe nicer than when he lived there. The last rain has helped. The grass is growing along the back gate, and the lime tree he planted four years ago finally has fruit. He still takes care of things around the house as if he lived there. He could pay the old man who cleans yards to come by, but it's still his house, still his family.

Corina and Little Jesse pull into the driveway a few minutes later. She hugs Jesse, but it's a hug you give an in-law or second cousin you don't see so often. Little Jesse gives his father a hug and then a high five the way he always does. Corina carries out a tray of sausages and marinated fajitas. She lingers around the pit while Jesse places the meat on the grill. Jesse can feel her watching him. He waits, knowing she has something to tell him. He covers the grill and watches the smoke escape through the vent.

It isn't until they're serving themselves the food that she brings up the idea of sending Little Jesse to another school. This, Jesse thinks, has to be the easiest decision they ever made. They live only a block away from an elementary school and Little Jesse is going into the second grade. What's there to talk about? Pack his lunch box and send him out the door. But now Corina has it in her head that Little Jesse needs to be going to the Catholic school across town.

"The books aren't any different over there, Corina. Schools are schools. Teachers are teachers."

"No, they're not. It's a better school, and you know it."

"No, I don't know what you're talking about. All I know is, we don't have money to be sending him there and especially not if he has a school right here."

"Gloria said she would help us pay."

"So this is your sister's idea?"

"She offered."

"All so he can go to class with a bunch of rich kids from her neighborhood?"

"She's not rich."

"She's richer than we are."

"It's a better school. That's the only reason."

"And how's he supposed to get there every day? In a taxi?"

"I'll take him on the way to work in the morning, and you can pick him up after school."

"I don't get off work until late in the afternoon, Corina."

"He can wait at Gloria's house until you come for him."

"And what if I don't want to? What if I say no?"

"Then I guess we have to do it without you."

Jesse knows the fight is officially over. It isn't the first time he's heard these words. Do it my way, or I'll do it myself. They hardly agreed on anything when he was living with her, sleeping in the same bed; how's it going to get any better with him living somewhere else?

Two months later, Jesse drives by Gloria's house and honks the horn. Gloria opens the front door and Little Jesse walks out, lugging his huge backpack. He climbs into the front seat of Jesse's small truck as though he's catching a ride with a passing 18-wheeler. Jesse plays with the stereo while Little Jesse straps himself in with the seat belt. "So, how was your first day?" Jesse asks. "Okay," Little Jesse answers. Jesse doesn't ask any more, but for what they're paying and the trouble of driving him back and forth, he thinks his first day should've been better than "okay."

Little Jesse is wearing a school uniform. His shirt is white with short sleeves and a button-down collar. It looks as though Corina used extra starch to make the shirt so stiff. Jesse tries to think of the last time she ironed anything for him, but he can only remember the time that she left a burn mark on his Polo shirt. Little Jesse's pants are gray with pleats and cuffs. His socks are as black as his shoes, which look as though they were polished at one of the stands across the river. They're buffed up enough that it's hard to tell what exactly is different about the left shoe. Jesse's waiting at a stoplight when he notices his own khakis are beginning to fade. His white shirt is missing a middle button, which his tie covers up. He realizes he should've worn something nicer.

He's an assistant manager now. They get all kinds of people walking in from the mall. The owner of Frontera Electronics is a businessman from Monterrey. He notices these kinds of things. Jesse knows that if he ever plans to be manager, it isn't going to happen with him missing a button on his shirt.

He drives Little Jesse back to the house. It's Monday and Corina will be at Dr. Rosas's office until five. She works as an assistant dental hygienist and takes classes at the college on the side. If she isn't rushing somewhere, she's studying or falling asleep from studying. Before he moved out, Jesse felt as if he were living in a school library because she kept saying "shush" anytime he listened to his music or talked on the phone. When he got tired of being shushed, he'd go hang out in the yard, where could make all the noise he wanted.

Little Jesse sits at the kitchen table and does his homework. Jesse serves them each a grape jelly sandwich with a glass of milk. Then he turns on the TV and watches a game show. A housewife from Minnesota has won a trip to Hawaii. She's jumping up and down, kissing her husband while the host asks if she's planning to take anyone on the trip. The audience laughs along with the wife and her husband.

"Mommy doesn't like the TV to be on when I do my homework."

"Why not?" Jesse says.

"She says I'll get distracted."

"What's she do then, when you're doing homework?"

"Read her books or make food for dinner. Or help me study."

"I don't have anything to read and I'm not that good a cook."

"Do you want to study with me?"

"Maybe you should wait for your mom."

Little Jesse shrugs in a way that says he has homework to do either way. He writes something in a blue notebook. Jesse clicks off the TV and leans back on the sofa. Little Jesse is reading out loud to himself. Jesse can hear the neighborhood boys shouting and playing football in the street. He falls asleep remembering one afternoon when he scored five touchdowns, two of them sprinting alongside the edge of the curb. He wakes up a few minutes later when Corina comes home and it's time for him to leave.

Jesse likes to stay in the truck when he goes by for Little Jesse. He waves hello to Gloria and leaves it at that. Weeks pass by this way. He doesn't have anything against Corina's family, but he knows they don't feel the same way about him since he moved out. It's not as if they really liked him to begin with. Corina met Jesse the summer she turned nineteen and was about to start college. She wanted to finish in three years and go to dental school in San Antonio. Jesse was eighteen years old, but he told her he was nineteen so she wouldn't think he was too young. Corina believed him until the day she saw his driver's license, but by that time they were going around. Jesse wasn't sure what he wanted to do. It was either join the air force or move to California and hang out with his older brother who sold vitamins and said he could set Jesse up. He thought he might go to college after the service. He wanted to leave his options open. Then Corina told him she was pregnant. But what really surprised him was that she wasn't sure she wanted to go through with it — the baby, or the marrying part. She said she loved him, but she just didn't know what to do. Her mind was full of all kinds of doubts. Where would they live? How would they survive? Did he want to marry her only because she was pregnant and he felt he had to? Maybe she was scared, maybe it was her family telling her it was the biggest mistake she'd ever make.

"Okay," Jesse told her. "If you don't want to have the baby, then don't. I'll take you to the clinic and pay for it."

"You will?"

"Yeah, but if you really love me, then you have to promise me one thing."

"What?"

"That right afterwards, you and me get married anyway."

His words were enough to convince her to marry him. The wedding took place during her fifth month, right before she started to show too much.

Jesse doesn't blame her family for feeling the way they do about him. He wouldn't like a guy like himself, either, especially now. Corina's family is made up of people who get married and stay married. Two of her brothers are lawyers and live in San Antonio with their families. Another brother is a dentist who lives and works with his wife in Houston. Corina and her sister are the only ones who stayed in Brownsville. Gloria married an older man who's a Customs supervisor at the bridge. They can't have kids, which is why they have the extra money to help out with Little Jesse's school. Their house backs up to a resaca and they have these ducks walking around the yard almost every day. Gloria feeds them and has a name for each one. The ducks are the one thing Little Jesse will go outside for. He throws a piece of bread at them and then rushes back to the patio as fast as he can, waving his arms in the air and screaming as if the birds were chasing after him. He waits a few seconds and does the whole thing over again.

Jesse is at home watching TV when the phone rings. It's Corina. She says Little Jesse made straight A's on his first report card and she thinks Jesse should do something special to celebrate. Jesse says okay — "Yeah, no problem" — but when he hangs up he has no idea what "something special" might be. He and Little Jesse haven't done anything special since he moved out. The rest of the night it's on his mind. The next morning at work, he still hasn't stopped thinking about what to do. They have a dozen TV sets on the floor and he turns them all to a kids' channel. Usually he can't stand the cartoons and the junior detective shows, but he's watching the commercials to see if he can come up with any ideas. The only thing he sees that they could do is the kiddie pizza place they went to once for Little Jesse's birthday. Jesse swore he'd never spend another afternoon there: big stuffed animals walking around trying to shake your hand, birthday boys and girls running everywhere, screaming, their parents letting them go wild. He clicks one of the TV sets and they have a show about polar bears. For a second, he thinks about going to the zoo, but he remembers the last time they went Little Jesse wore himself out before they reached the petting zoo, and then he had to carry him on his back the rest of the afternoon because the kid didn't want to get in a stroller.

After lunch, when he still hasn't come up with anything, he asks Mary Lou, the cashier, where she would take a kid. She's always talking about her four boys. She should know.

"Take him to play video games," Mary Lou tells him.

"Nah, he doesn't like them that much," Jesse says.

"¿Cómo qué, he doesn't like them? Everybody plays those games."

"He likes to read books."

Mary Lou shakes her head in disbelief.

"Why don't you take him to ride the little ponies at the flea market?"

"He doesn't like to be outside."

"He doesn't like to be outside?" she says. "N'hombre, mine would sleep outside if I let them."

"That's the way I was when I was a kid."

"What's he like to do then?"

"Nothing," Jesse says. "That's the problem. Nothing."

When he picks up Little Jesse that afternoon, he's still not sure what they'll do to celebrate. He thinks about asking Little Jesse, but he's afraid he might say pizza. Finally, he decides to take him to the movies. Jesse buys tickets to a movie about some talking dogs, nothing he would ever pay to see on his own, but at least it's cheaper in the afternoon. He loads Little Jesse up on buttered popcorn and Coke. "Just don't tell Mommy, okay?" Jesse says as they take their seats. He knows Corina never lets the kid drink soda, doesn't keep it in the house, and he hopes buying one now might be a small clue to his son that his father isn't such a bad guy.

"Did you like the movie?" Jesse asks after they're back in the truck.

"I liked the little one."

"Wienie dogs are always funny, no matter what."

"They're called dachshunds. I saw it in the encyclopedia."

"You can call them whatever you want, they're still wienie dogs to me."

Little Jesse is quiet after this. He seems to be thinking about what his father said.

"Can some dogs really talk?" Little Jesse asks.

"Only to other dogs." And then Jesse barks.

Little Jesse looks at his father for a second and starts laughing. The rest of the ride home, Jesse answers all of Little Jesse's questions with a bark.

Corina hasn't forgiven Jesse for something he did. It happened the summer Little Jesse turned four. Jesse and Little Jesse were walking through the parking lot at the mall when the boy stopped to look at a motorcycle. He stared at his reflection in the chrome, smiled, and reached out to touch the muffler. Jesse saw him at the last second and yelled louder than he'd ever yelled in his life. He grabbed Little Jesse's arm and yanked it away before he touched anything. Little Jesse started crying that second and didn't stop until after they were home. Jesse felt he had to defend himself the more the kid cried. When he finally did stop crying, he threw up on his pillow. Corina held him the whole time, but Jesse could see she was already accusing him with her eyes.

"Why weren't you holding his hand?"

"I was holding it."

"If you were holding it, this wouldn't have happened."

"Okay, but nothing happened. Look at him, he didn't get burned or nothing."

"He threw up, Jesse."

"That's not my fault."

"Did you hit him?"

"I pulled him away, Corina, that's all."

"Did you yell at him?"

"Just so he wouldn't touch the muffler. Just to stop him."

"What about in the truck?"

"What about it?"

"Did you yell at him?"

"There was no yelling, there was only him crying. He wouldn't have heard me back there anyway."

"Back there where?"

"In the back of the truck. I told you, he wouldn't stop crying."

"You put him in the camper of the truck?"

"He's ridden back there before. He likes it."

Corina didn't talk to Jesse for more than a week. At first, he couldn't understand what she was so pissed off about. The kid had been crying and screaming. Jesse tried to hold him the way he'd seen Corina do when he fell. He thought maybe Little Jesse had touched the muffler and he hadn't seen it, but his hand was fine, no marks or anything. Jesse told him he was sorry for yelling. He told him it was all over now and they were going home. They could watch videos or read his books, anything. He told Little Jesse that if he stopped crying, he'd take him to the raspa stand that was close to the house and buy him whatever flavor he wanted. But nothing worked. Jesse thought he was going to go crazy with all the crying. He wished Brownsville wasn't so damn flat because he wanted to drive off a cliff. If Little Jesse wasn't crying, he was screaming. If he wasn't screaming, he was crying. Back and forth like that, back and forth, back and forth, until Jesse couldn't take it anymore and carried him to the camper.

Now thinking it over, there's no doubt in his mind that in a court of law he would be found guilty and sent to wherever it is they send bad fathers — in his case, to an efficiency apartment located three miles from the house where his family lives. And in this 400-square-foot box, he thinks about that afternoon and wonders if it would've been better if Little Jesse had touched the muffler. At least if he had fried his little hand, there would've been something to really make him cry and for Jesse to feel bad about. But he had stopped him from burning his hand and tried to make him stop crying. He did all this, and still he's doing his time. He also thinks about Corina's question of why he wasn't holding Little Jesse's hand, but he hasn't come up with a good answer. He wishes he could say that his hands were full of bags or that he only let go of him right in front of the car, but both of these would be lies. The only reason he's come up with for not holding his hand is that he didn't want to baby him the way Corina does. He wanted him to be strong. He wanted him to be normal.

It's taken some time for Jesse to get used to being alone in the apartment. He moved straight from his mother's house to the house where he lived with Corina and then to his small apartment, where it's just him. Jesse moved in with zero furniture and had to borrow a plastic lawn chair because he was tired of sitting on the floor or on top of the toilet seat cover anytime he wanted to tie his shoes. He picked up the mattress at a clearance sale. And he bought the TV for almost nothing because the wood paneling had been scratched on the floor. Little by little, he's getting more comfortable in the apartment.

Jesse can make anything with eggs: frijoles con huevo, chorizo con huevo, ham and eggs, bacon and eggs, potato and eggs. Making hamburgers on the stove isn't that different from grilling them outside. He borrowed two pots and a pan when he left. The smaller pot he uses to heat up vegetables. The big pot is for cooking beans or spaghetti. The pan is for making eggs or hamburgers or heating up tortillas. So far, he doesn't have any plates or silverware, but this has worked out because it means he uses paper plates and plastic forks and never has to wash dishes.

When he eats out, he usually goes to Reyna's Café. He knows Reyna because he eats breakfast there a few times a week, but their conversations are limited to the weather and how business is for the restaurant or the store. She doesn't know about Jesse's problems at home, and he'd rather keep it that way. He goes there for the breakfast, not counseling. They have a special every morning: two eggs, beans, a slice of bacon, and a flour tortilla for $2.50. Coffee is extra. Jesse shows up early, when it's usually quiet and there are only other men eating their breakfasts alone and reading the *Herald* or *El Bravo*. It gets louder about eight, when the bigger tables begin to fill up.

This morning he's sitting at the counter. The restaurant is busy for it being early. One of the bigger tables is filled with a group of Border Patrol agents, their walkie-talkies standing guard next to the salt and pepper shakers. Four businessmen sit at a table near the back wall and laugh about the one man who didn't show up because his wife doesn't let him out of bed this early. An older man and a young woman are nudged up against each other in a booth, both of them paying more attention to what he's whispering in her ear than to the food in front of them. Jesse is eating a machacado con huevo taco so big that the edges of the tortilla hang over the side of the platter. Halfway through his breakfast, the doorbells jingle and a little man walks into the restaurant. He's little enough that no one is sure if he's just a really short man or a tall midget. If it weren't for the faint whiskers sprouting above his lip, he'd pass for a seven-year-old boy. Most of the people in the place

BROWNSVILLE

turn around in their seats and stare until they get their fill of
him. Reyna walks out from behind the counter. She's smiling
and serving coffee, but she doesn't take her eyes off the new
customer who just walked in. A little girl at a center table gig-
gles and asks her mother if they can take the toy man home.
The mother quiets the girl, but they both keep looking at him
as he walks around the restaurant. Jesse is taking the last bite
of his tortillia when the little guy hands him a card that says
he's deaf and mute and can you please help him out with a
dollar donation. The back side of the card has hand signals for
the Spanish alphabet. About half the people give him a dollar;
the other half ignore him as though he were a fly that's been let
inside the door. An elderly woman hands him two dollars and
then reaches out and touches his cheek. It crosses Jesse's mind
that the guy might be lying about being deaf and mute. He's
heard of people scamming money this way, pretending to be
mudos when they can talk like everybody else. Either way,
Jesse gives him a dollar for being born a shorty. It's the one
thing he knows the guy isn't faking. After the man pockets the
dollar, he holds up his bony little hand and makes the sign of
the cross over Jesse.

Jesse sticks around the restaurant drinking an extra cup of
coffee. He wonders where the little guy came from and if his
parents were midgets. If they were small, would they have
been happy with a regular-size baby? Corina and Jesse didn't
notice any real difference when they first came home from the
hospital. Their baby was like any other baby, laughing, crying, crawling, getting into things. It wasn't until he stood in

the playpen that they noticed anything. The doctor told them about a procedure to stretch Little Jesse's leg, but they'd have to wait until his bones grew more. In the meantime, a shoe lift would help make up the difference. Jesse remembers at first wanting to blame the doctor. And the more he thought about it, he blamed himself, except he didn't know what for — his genes, his blood, his partying too much when he was younger. For a while, he blamed God. Then he blamed himself all over again. But he couldn't understand what he had done in eighteen years to deserve this. Corina only blamed herself, never really believing the doctors who told her there was nothing she could've done. Jesse used to help Corina with the baby at night. Sometimes he'd walk around the house, carrying him until Little Jesse fell asleep; other times, he'd sit in the recliner and give him his bottle. After the baby fell asleep, Jesse would massage his shorter leg. He pulled on the skinny thigh and calf as though he were trying to pull off a long sock, thinking that maybe if he kept doing it, his legs would be the same length by the time he started walking and they wouldn't have to take him back to the doctor. And later, when Little Jesse kept falling, Jesse told himself he was only getting his balance the way all babies did. The worst was hearing other people, especially women, say, "Ay, pobrecito," every time he fell. He knew Corina had carried Little Jesse because she didn't want him to hurt himself. But Jesse carried him because he didn't want people to know their baby wasn't like a regular baby. Of all the things he's done, this is the only one he's ashamed of.

Jesse is closing for Mary Lou. She asked for the night off so she and her husband could take their kids to the carnival. It reminds Jesse of how when he was a kid he couldn't wait for the carnival to come to town. He used to walk all over the neighborhood collecting aluminum cans to make enough money for the rides and games. Once he rode the Zipper seven times in a single night. Another year he won a Kiss poster at a booth and hung it on the wall in his room. He keeps thinking about all those times until he finally phones Corina to say he wants to take her and Little Jesse to the carnival. Corina says she's taking Little Jesse to the children's parade, but she thinks he's still too young for the carnival, and besides, there are always too many people.

"That's what carnivals are for, Corina — people, families."

"I don't think he's going to like the rides."

"What six-year-old doesn't like rides?"

Two nights later, Jesse drives by the house to take them out. He treats them to Pizza Hut first. Little Jesse likes the pizza but wants to know why there aren't any big stuffed animals walking around. "Big-people pizza," Jesse tells him. "You're a big boy now, aren't you?" Little Jesse nods and takes another bite. Corina seems happy at first, but she doesn't like it when Jesse orders beer. "I'm not drinking," she says. Jesse pours her beer back into the pitcher. "Whatever you want, Corina. Whatever."

Jesse isn't going to let her ruin the night, even when she happens to be right about there being a lot of people at the carnival. So what? They're at the carnival. Rock music is blaring out of giant speakers next to the Himalaya roller coaster. The only thing louder is the screaming of young girls begging to get off the rides. Jesse can't remember the last time he was at a carnival. He can tell that Little Jesse is having fun and likes the rides. Jesse doesn't care that they're all kiddie rides, either. He buys his boy cotton candy and lets him throw away money on a game where he has to pop balloons with darts. Five dollars later, Little Jesse hasn't hit one balloon, but it still doesn't matter. They're all laughing and having a good time.

After a while, Little Jesse says he wants to ride the bumper cars, but Corina thinks the line is too long and they should wait for another time. "Another time won't come until next year," Jesse says and grabs Little Jesse's hand.

They wait in line behind the other fathers and sons. After watching the bumper cars slam into each other for a few minutes, Jesse notices the father and son in front of him both have rattails. Rata and Rata Jr., he thinks to himself. Jesse imagines the father and son sitting next to each other in barber chairs and telling the barber they want the exact same haircut. He can see them spinning around afterward and checking themselves out in the mirror, each one reaching back to play with his colita. Rata Jr. looks like a perfect copy of his dad, only smaller and without the homemade tattoos and fresh love marks on his neck. Jesse laughs a little, still feeling kind of buzzed from earlier. Right then, Rata turns to look back at Jesse but doesn't say anything, just looks at him hard. For a second, Jesse thinks the guy might have heard him laughing. Rata finally cocks his head back to say hello. Jesse does the

same back to him. He knows this is the main reason Corina
didn't want to come to the carnival. When she said there were
"too many people," what she really meant was that there
were too many people like Rata.

They're almost at the head of the line when Rata Jr.
reaches over and grabs a piece of Little Jesse's cotton candy.
Little Jesse turns away, but the kid does it again. The third
time it happens, Little Jesse looks up at Jesse as if he needs instructions on what to do next. Jesse finally takes the cotton
candy away so Rata Jr. can't reach it. He's holding it above
his own head when Rata turns around.

"Hey, bro', why do you have be so pinche?" Rata says.
"It's just some cotton candy."

"Go buy yourself some then. They sell it over there."

"What, you think your boy's too good to share?"

Jesse's about to say something about how he doesn't want
his son catching any rat diseases, but the gate opens and it's
their turn for the ride. Little Jesse climbs into a red bumper
car with a white racing stripe down the middle. Corina is
waiting along the railing and Jesse can hear her yelling at him
to get inside one of the cars, but he pretends not to hear her.
He helps Little Jesse get strapped in and then walks to where
Corina is standing.

"He's too little to be doing it alone," she says.

"No he's not, Corina. Look at the other kids."

She shakes her head, but Jesse is busy waving at their son.

Little Jesse smiles and waves as he drives the bumper car
in a half circle. He's still saying hi when Rata Jr. rams his car
from behind. Little Jesse laughs and tries to bump him back,

but he doesn't turn the steering wheel fast enough and Rata Jr. hits him again.

"Hit him back!" Jesse yells. "You can do it!"

Little Jesse looks up long enough that he doesn't see the bumper car coming at him from another angle. Jesse can hear Rata laughing only a few feet away. "Like that, Junior, like that. ¡Chíngatelo!"

Jesse tries to ignore Rata at first.

"Hey, bro'," Rata says. "Your boy don't know how to drive. Where'd he get his driver's license? Matamoros?"

"Nobody's talking to you, man."

"Oyes, güey, don't get all pissed off just 'cause your boy can't drive for shit."

Corina pulls on Jesse's arm. "Leave him alone," she whispers. "It's not worth it."

"He's the one talking to me."

"Leave him, Jesse."

Little Jesse lets go of the steering wheel and waves his hands in the air. He's looking everywhere for Corina and Jesse. His lower lip is quivering the way it does right before he begins crying and screaming.

"Go get him," Corina says.

"How? The ride's not finished."

"Tell them to stop the ride, that you need to get your son."

"He'll be all right, Corina."

But Jesse knows this isn't true. Some other kids bump into Little Jesse's car and he's stuck in the far corner of the floor. He's crying out for Corina now. She climbs over the rail and onto the metal floor before the ride stops. Jesse doesn't know what's worse, watching Corina rescue him or watching him cry in front of everyone.

Rata Jr. slams into Little Jesse one last time before Corina gets to him.

"Ya déjalo, Junior," Rata yells. "He's a baby. He can't even reach the gas pedal with his leg."

Jesse wishes he hadn't heard these words. He feels as if he's on one of the carnival rides and the momentum is taking his body. He can't stop himself. He shoves Rata against the rail. He wants to yell at him, call him a son of a bitch, a fuck- ing asshole, a puto, but he's choking on the words.

Rata turns around and backs up. "¡Orale, pendejo! You want some shit with me?"

It's over almost as soon as it starts, not because Jesse kicks his ass the way he wants to or because Rata shows him what he did to the last guy who was stupid enough to lay a hand on him, but because a couple of cops walk by and see them fighting in the grass. One of the cops pins Rata to the ground, facedown, and handcuffs him. The other one pulls Jesse away and slams him against the bumper car railing before hand- cuffing him.

The first cop stands Rata up and leads him toward the front gate. The other cop waits until they've left before he turns Jesse around from the railing. A small crowd has gath- ered. One father is holding his son on his shoulders. A skinny carnival worker wearing red suspenders is standing next to a milk bottle game. He spits a long brown stream of tobacco juice into the grass. A large woman in a flannel shirt watches while she eats a candy apple. A young boyfriend holds his girlfriend from behind, his arms slung over her shoulders and the letterman jacket she's wearing. All these eyes bear down on Jesse. He feels as though he doesn't exist anymore. He's just a guy who started a fight with another guy, a couple of strangers these people will remember years from now when they think about the carnival. His right cheek feels bruised and he can taste a little blood from the cut on his lip. His shirt is ripped open and his jeans have grass stains at the knees. His right shoe slipped off when he and Rata were on the ground. He feels the dry grass pricking his foot.

Jesse looks around for Corina and Little Jesse, but he sees only blank eyes staring back at him. Everything in the carnival seems bigger than it was before. The Zipper towers above, each end rising and disappearing into a starless sky. The Moon Walk looks inflated enough that it might float away with all the kids tumbling around inside of it. The cop begins to lead Jesse away. A river of people moves past them on either side. Off to the left, Jesse sees Corina standing next to the House of Mirrors. She's holding Little Jesse next to her and turning his face so he doesn't see his father.

Jesse knows he did the right thing, standing up for his son. He tells himself that any father would've done the same. Corina won't see it this way, though. She'll say that he has to grow up already and stop acting like he's eighteen and that if he really cared about Little Jesse, he would've taken him out of the bumper car and not paid attention to Rata. Jesse can already hear her. She'll say he only started the fight because he's too proud, which is what he always thought fathers were supposed to be of their sons. Proud.

The crowd of people has almost doubled now. Some of the men in back are pushing as though they've paid to enter a sideshow, the chance to see a real bearded woman or a three-headed goat. A couple of people in the crowd are pointing at Jesse. A woman holding a little boy by the hand shouts out in Spanish that this is a carnival, not a wrestling match. If he wants to fight, he should go on *Lucha Libre*. The crowd laughs. Someone else yells out that he needs to put on a mask if he really wants to be Mil Mascaras. They laugh some more. The crowd parts as the cop leads him toward the entrance. Jesse searches for Corina and Little Jesse along the way, but he sees only strangers staring back at him. A teenage boy has Jesse's other shoe and he's waving it in the air like it's a prize he won. Jesse wore his old brown shoes because he didn't have to worry about keeping them clean. They're scuffed up and the laces busted years ago. These are his shoes for working in the yard or cooking out or taking his kid to the carnival. He wants to ask for his shoe, but the cop is tugging at him. Jesse steps awkwardly every time his right foot comes down. It looks as though he's stepping into a small hole and then out of it again with his next stride. People are laughing at the way he's walking and telling him not to forget his shoe, that he'll need it when he gets out of jail. The boy with the shoe mimics the way Jesse walks, making him look more like a chimp than a man. This gets the biggest laughs so far. Jesse could step on his toes and look like anyone else walking out of a carnival. But he doesn't. He lets them keep laughing. It's the only thing he can hear now.

Charro

Marcelo Torres was running away from a large barking dog that was about to bite him. The dog was foaming at the mouth, and Marcelo could feel it spitting on him each time its jaws snapped shut. He couldn't understand why the hell he hadn't worn more than his boxers. It was late at night and his neighbors were watching him through their window blinds. Marcelo ran and ran, but he moved as though he were waist deep in a river. And right when the animal was about to bite down, when Marcelo could feel its hot, rabid breath on his legs, he woke up and realized that it was only a dream but that the barking dog was real and outside his window. It was 3:30 in the morning.

Marcelo walked to his neighbor's house after work the next day. Someone else might have settled the matter by calmly explaining the situation, but Marcelo Torres wasn't a man who spoke with soft or tactful words. He didn't speak this way on the ranch where he'd lived before he was married and moved to the city. He didn't speak this way at work as a livestock inspector for the USDA. And you can be sure he didn't speak this way when somebody's dog wouldn't stop barking outside his window in the middle of the night.

He banged on the screen door and it rattled on its hinges. One of the Sanchez boys, a fat kid with a crew cut, opened the door holding a fish stick covered in ketchup.

"Where's your father?"

The little boy ran to the kitchen. Marcelo heard voices and then the boy came back, still holding the fish stick.

"My father says if you can come later. He's eating supper."

"Tell your father I want to talk to him now."

The boy hurried back to the kitchen and there were more voices. Marcelo was waiting on the porch when the dog came by and sniffed his pants. It went up the right leg and down the left, as if it were frisking a suspect. The dog was a German shepherd and chow mix. Its fur was a thick forest of black and reddish brown hair. The full mane was the chow part and the low, slanting back and long hind legs were the German shepherd part. When it licked the top of his boots, Marcelo noticed its tongue was the color of a dark bruise. He pushed the animal aside with his knee. For the past two nights it had been barking in his yard. Olivia and the boys hadn't had any trouble sleeping through this, which only frustrated him more when he was wide awake and listening to the dog. He figured he'd lost two or three hours of sleep because of the barking.

Marcelo waited a minute and yelled, "Sanchez!" through the screen door. He heard furniture scraping on the floor and his neighbor walking toward him. Sanchez owned a lawn mower repair shop that he ran out of his backyard. He was a short, round man who wore thick glasses, beige khakis, and a white V neck shirt to work every day. His thin leather belt split his large gut into two separate bellies.

"¿Qué fue, Torres?" They were looking at each other, eye to eye, through the screen door.

"Your dog, Sanchez."

"Charro? No, pues, he really belongs to my boys. They found him over there in the park. They say he was lost."

"Why didn't you call the pound?"

"¿N'hombre, pa'qué? He's a good dog."

"He barks a lot."

"That's what dogs do, they bark. Did you hear somebody stole one of my machines the other day? A Sears power mower, cost me eighty dollars."

"Sanchez, I didn't walk over here to talk about your lawn mowers."

"Then what?"

"Your dog's been barking in my yard at night."

"He's just getting used to the neighborhood, Torres. I think he likes it here. It makes him happy, le da gusto, and he barks."

"I don't care why the hell he's barking, Sanchez. He could've won the lottery and I still wouldn't care."

"Why you getting mad, Torres? I can't help it if Charro hears things. You should be glad he protects the neighborhood."

"All I know is, you better do something to shut that animal up. People got to sleep."

"Nobody else is complaining. You're the only one, Torres."

"Yeah, and I'm going to be the one calling the pound if I hear it barking again."

Marcelo turned and walked off. He heard Sanchez saying Charro was just a dog and didn't know better, but he only raised his hand and swatted the words away as though they were flies.

The barking stopped that night. Marcelo woke up satisfied that Sanchez had done something to control his dog. For a while he had considered extending the wooden fence he already had in the backyard, but they weren't giving away fences and he wasn't about to pay for one because of Sanchez's dog.

The peace and quiet ended a few nights later. The dog trapped something underneath the house and all the barking roused Marcelo out of his sleep. He pushed hard on the window until it cracked open.

"Marcelo, what are you doing?"

"Nada, Olivia, the dog won't stop barking."

He leaned on the windowsill with both hands and pressed his face against the screen. "¡Perro chingado, cállate el hocico!"

"Marcelo, people are sleeping."

"Ya déjame, por favor, Olivia. This is between me and that damn dog."

The dog stared straight at him and kept barking, only louder now. Marcelo felt his way around the dark bedroom. He groped inside the closet and grabbed the first thing he touched. Then he unlatched the screen window and flung a boot into the yard. The heel caught the dog on the back of the head and it ran off crying. Marcelo laughed.

"What's the matter, happy dog?" he shouted out the window. "You don't feel like barking? Andale, cabrón. No more bow-wow for you tonight."

It was in the early morning, when Marcelo was leaving for work, that he found several chewed pieces of his calfskin boot scattered around the front yard, some of them still wet with dog saliva.

Sanchez claimed that his dog must have crawled under the fence. He said he'd been chaining it to a tree, but the kids kept teasing the poor animal. They would play with it by the tree, and the dog would chase after them until the chain yanked it back. He was afraid Charro was going to get hurt and have to go to the animal doctor. Anyway, he was sorry about the boot, but what could he do? It was a dog.

"You can buy me some new boots, Sanchez, that's what you can do. Those were handmade in Monterrey."

But Sanchez said he couldn't afford to buy his own kids new shoes. How was he going to buy him some fancy cowboy boots? It wouldn't be right. Besides, it wasn't exactly his fault. He didn't throw the boot; he didn't chew it up. The dog was probably just playing.

"That's how they play."

"Sanchez, you better hope I don't find your stupid dog

playing in my yard." Marcelo walked away from his neighbor's porch.

"Torres . . ."

"To hell with you, Sanchez!"

"Torres . . ."

"And to hell with that pinche perro of yours."

The next day was Sunday, the day he had promised to take Olivia and the boys to church and to visit her mother's grave in the upper Valley. This was always a sacrifice for Marcelo since her family had never cared for him. The mother had been of the opinion that her only daughter could have done better than to marry a man who was twelve years older and raised in the country. She never accepted that he'd walked away from that world, from everything he knew, in order to provide a better life for her daughter.

Marcelo had lived most of his life on El Rancho Capote, where his father had taught him how to work. The ranch was located northwest of Brownsville, along a small bend in the Rio Grande. Now his government job provided him with a decent salary and medical benefits for the family: Marcelo, Olivia, Junior, and the baby, Arturo. He spent his days — whether it was 102 degrees outside or pouring rain — checking on ranches and farms in the county, answering calls about stray animals, spraying livestock for ticks and other diseases, and patrolling the river on horseback to stop animals from being smuggled into the U.S. He'd been shot at three different times when he accidentally rode into brushy areas where drugs were being crossed over. One of Marcelo's good friends was chasing a stray calf when his horse fell into the river. Ed Zamora's body was dragged out by the county the next morning. Some of the men complained about having to patrol the river, but Marcelo wasn't one of them. He'd ridden practically every twisting mile from Santa Maria to the mouth of the river. He had never met the women who washed their clothes along the banks on the other side, but he waved to them every day. He could tell you where the currents weren't as dangerous and people were most likely to cross and fight their way through the tall grass near the levee, half dressed with their dry clothes in hand. He didn't bother them, and they didn't bother him. But mainly, the long rides along the river gave Marcelo time to go over his life, how he'd been raised to live and work on a ranch, but now he had a job where he only visited ranches and always in a light green truck marked USDA.

He had been doing this work for almost fourteen years. Olivia's mother used to tell people that he was like a dog-catcher for large animals. But this Sunday he tried to put aside his feelings. At first he had wanted to tell Olivia that he didn't feel like spending the afternoon visiting her mother, except he knew she'd be disappointed. He held the words in his chest, refusing to let them come to the surface.

After church, Marcelo stopped at the Fina station to fill the tank for the long drive to the cemetery. He was nearly on empty. The station had switched over to self-service a year earlier, but he had avoided stopping there because he hated these new places that didn't offer at least some service. He thought they owed people a little more for their money. Olivia stayed in the car with the boys, and Marcelo filled the Oldsmobile's tank. He looked down at his clothes while he pumped the gas. He'd felt uncomfortable wearing his old boots in church. The leather was cracked and the heels were worn down along the edges. During mass he noticed he'd missed a spot when he was cleaning them that morning. He was so distracted that he couldn't find anything to pray for except patience during the drive to the cemetery.

Marcelo had already finished filling the tank when he saw the attendant talking on the phone behind the counter. He was a teenager, maybe fifteen or sixteen years at the most, wearing a baseball cap backwards.

"¡Eh!" Marcelo said. He was holding the money in the air. The attendant didn't hear and turned his back to Marcelo.

He tried whistling to get his attention. If the boy was going to pretend to be as dumb as a farm animal, he'd treat him that way. The kid finally turned around when he heard the high-pitched whistle, but he didn't hang up the phone. Marcelo felt some bitter words rise in his throat.

"Hey, who do you think I'm talking to? You think I'm here because I like the smell of gasoline? ¿Crees qué estoy loco o qué? Get out here, güerco arrastrado! Or you want me to drag you out here with that phone? I'm talking to you. Yeah, you!"

The teenager put down the phone when he realized that the crazy man waving the dollar bills was actually yelling at him. Olivia told the boys to sit back and stop staring at their father. Junior, the older boy, was already rolling down the window. The attendant stood inside the doorway and refused to step outside for the money. Marcelo finally stuffed the end of the dollar bills inside the gas pump and stuck the nozzle right in after them. He started up the Oldsmobile and drove to the cemetery without saying another word for the rest of the trip.

The dog stopped coming to Marcelo's window at night. He only heard it barking from a distance as it ran through the neighborhood. When he called the police in the morning, they told him the city answered complaints only if the animal was threatening people. The woman at the dog pound said they'd send someone over, but if the dog was in its yard during the day, there was nothing they could do.

These days Marcelo was patrolling a few miles from the mouth of the river. He had to be careful in the areas where the bank dropped off and the trail continued again a little farther downstream. If he wasn't in a hurry, he might stop in the shade and watch the men on the other side of the river herding their cattle from one pasture to another. Some of the men had dogs to help them with the cattle. Marcelo's father used to have a dog that killed rattlesnakes. The dog would bite a snake in the midsection and pound its head against the ground until it died. The dog survived more than a few bites over the years and finally passed away from old age. Marcelo laughed when he imagined Sanchez's dog on the ranch. It wouldn't have lasted a day. Animals had to work for their food like everyone else. It didn't matter what Sanchez said, the dog wasn't protecting his lawn mowers or the neighborhood. What the dog needed was to learn a lesson or two about respect.

One Saturday morning Marcelo woke up early to work around the house. Olivia and the boys were sleeping late. He had planned to clean out the carport, but when he walked outside he saw Charro sleeping by the Oldsmobile. Marcelo was about to grab a stick and show the animal how welcome it was on his property, but he thought of a better idea. He walked back inside and grabbed two wienies out of the refrigerator. The dog swallowed the first wienie in one bite. Marcelo dangled the second one higher than the dog could reach. It leaped several times but never high enough. Then he opened the trunk of the car and tossed the wienie inside. Charro jumped in after it, and Marcelo shut the trunk.

He drove on International with the radio turned to his favorite station. A few minutes later he was feeling the heavy rhythm of his tires rolling over the deep cracks on State Highway 4, the narrow two-lane road that followed the Rio Grande until it became the Gulf. Like most mornings, there was hardly any traffic. Dark gray clouds hung low over the flat brushland on both sides of the highway. Marcelo saw only two animals along the road. The first was a hawk perched on a rotting mesquite. He honked a couple of times to see if he could scare the bird into spreading its wings and flying off, but it stayed where it had landed. Later he drove around a bend in the road and had to swerve in order to miss what he guessed was a dead coyote, although by then it didn't look like anything that had ever been alive. The highway ended more than twenty miles from the city limits. Marcelo drove from the pavement onto the sand at Boca Chica. The beach was deserted except for a rusted-out washer and dryer, a torched car, dirty Pampers, and the rest of the junk people always dumped there. Marcelo rolled down the window and let the Gulf breeze fill the car. He drove along the shore with his arm sticking out the window as he listened to his polkas. And at the farthest point — where there was no sign of life but an abandoned beach house that had somehow survived the last few hurricanes, where the jetty rose from the sand with jagged blocks of concrete, and where a quarter mile of choppy sea water separated this lonely beach from the resort hotels on South Padre Island — Marcelo stopped the car.

He pulled the dog out of the trunk and it ran circles around him as though it wanted to play in the sand. "Ven pa'ca, perro desgraciado. Come on, here, dog."

It bolted in a different direction each time Marcelo went near it. He finally crouched on all fours to see if it would come closer. The dog turned its head to one side and stared at him as if it were looking into a mirror.

"Ven, Charro, ven."

The dog inched closer and he grabbed it long enough to slip off its leather collar and ID tags. Marcelo used his hands to help himself climb the rocks on the jetty. He flung the collar and tags into the water. They floated for a few seconds before they sank. When Marcelo walked back to the car, the dog was still in the mood to play and it jumped high enough to put its dirty paws on his chest. He knocked the animal down and kicked it in the stomach, but even that didn't stop it from chasing the car.

"¡Perro chingado, cállate el hocico!" Marcelo honked the horn over and over as he watched the dog fade to a tiny brown spot in his rearview mirror.

Two days passed before Sanchez knocked on Marcelo's front door. He brought his little boy. They came to ask if Marcelo had seen Charro. The boy was crying to himself and chewing on a piece of his father's pants. Marcelo felt sorry for him and said he was sure the dog would come back.

Sanchez walked over again the next day, this time alone.

"Ya te dije, Sanchez, I haven't seen your dog. What more do you want?"

"Torres, it's not my fault you don't like Charro."

"¿Y qué, everybody's supposed to love your dog? I'm supposed to like the little presents he leaves in my yard every night?"

"You can't say for sure it's Charro. There's other dogs."

"¿Mira, sabes qué? Next time I'll put it in a plastic bag and bring it over so you can look at it and tell me for sure."

"Torres, all I'm saying is that you might have seen what happened to him."

"Are you blaming me?" He opened the screen door, and Sanchez backed down off the porch.

"No."

"It sounds like you are. It sounds like you're standing in front of my house blaming me because your dog hasn't come home."

"I didn't say that."

"¿Entonces?"

"All I'm saying is that if you see him to call me."

"For what? So he can wake me up in the middle of the night again?"

"It's the boy's dog, Torres. Por favor, he misses his dog."

"Wait until he has a job and a family and see how much he misses the dog."

Marcelo thought he was dreaming when he heard the barking a week later. But looking out his bedroom window, he saw Charro staring straight at him. The dog was louder and more playful than before, as if its time away had been some sort of dog vacation.

Marcelo ran outside with a broom just as Charro was hiking a leg on his bougainvilleas. The dog moved before he could hit it, and his first swing went into the bushes. When he finally recovered the broom, the dog began running large circles around him. Marcelo swung wildly like a kid trying to hit a piñata at a birthday party. "¡Méndigo ... desgraciado ... sanavabiche!" he yelled out after each swing. He was getting closer to hitting the dog when it suddenly turned and chased a cat down the alley.

He walked back inside and rested on the bed. Olivia asked him what he was doing and he told her he'd been in the bathroom. She rolled over on her side and fell asleep. Part of him wanted to go back and look for the dog, but it was almost three o'clock in the morning. He stared at the ceiling and watched the fan go round and round. Another hour went by before he was able to fall asleep.

The next morning, Monday, he overslept and arrived late for work. He had to hear his supervisor tell him, in front of the other men, that if he couldn't be on time for their weekly meetings maybe they needed to talk. The room fell silent and all the men — except for Marcelo and the supervisor — looked down at the tips of their boots. Marcelo told him it wouldn't happen again.

Of all the things he'd learned over the years, he knew that playing around with a man's work was something you didn't do. Marcelo rode along the edge of the river for an extra hour that day. All he could think of was how he wasn't going to lose his job because of a dog. He remembered when he was fifteen and his family moved across the river to Reynosa. They'd been there a month when his father got into an argument with a man named Norberto Valdez. The men exchanged words after Valdez accused Marcelo's father of stealing some cattle. Valdez threatened to report the Torres family to the authorities and force them off their ranch. The fight that almost broke out ended with both men warning each other about the trouble they'd started. Back at the ranch, Marcelo's father gathered his sons, all five of them, and told them he was giving them each a gun. The first one to see Norberto Valdez was to shoot him. Benito, the oldest, was the lucky son. He spent ten years in the Reynosa jail. Nobody ever stopped to question whether it had been the right thing to do. All they knew was that their family had been threatened. Marcelo had to do something about the dog.

He stopped at Lopez Supermarket on the way home. The meat department was located at the back of the store, next to the milk and cheese. They were having a special on H&H chorizo, his favorite. The wienies had worked the first time, but he wanted to try something different. The meat cutter said the ground round was fresh and had been put out that afternoon. The steaks in the glass case looked nice and juicy, but they were kind of expensive. Marcelo thought about the past two months with the dog barking in the middle of the night and he asked himself how he would feel after giving it something to make it sick. Would he be able to sleep at night, knowing that he'd killed an animal, a little boy's dog? He couldn't exactly answer yes, but he didn't have any better ideas. He bought a medium-size package of ground round.

Marcelo finished off two servings of carne guisada for dinner. Olivia had made her famous rice and reheated some pinto beans from the day before. He thought her flour tortillas were the best he'd ever tasted and he told her again that night. After dinner, Marcelo said he needed to check if he'd locked the doors to the truck. The sun had been down for a couple of hours. He used his keys to unlock the toolbox. The narrow metal container was suspended from both sides directly behind the cab. On one side of the box he stored hammers, screwdrivers, wrenches, pliers, wire cutters, and a leather hole puncher. On the other side, sectioned off by a divider, he put away his bridles, bits, spurs, and leather gloves. This was also the side where he had hidden the meat.

He reached underneath the toolbox and pulled out a large brown jug filled with a chemical he used to spray livestock for ticks. The solution was mixed with water before the treatment was applied. The ingredients on the label stretched out into extra-long words that looked like a foreign language to

Marcelo. What he understood was the symbol of the skull and crossbones.

Blood squished between his fingers as he rolled the meat into four little balls the size of tangerines. With his pinky, he poked a small hole in each meatball and poured in as much of the chemical as he could. He covered the opening by rolling the meatball around in his hands until it was nice and smooth.

He lay awake in bed. Olivia was asleep. About 2:30 he heard Charro barking in the distance. The sound was getting closer by the minute. He heard the dog knock over what sounded like the Hinojosas' trash can. A few minutes later it cornered an alley cat, which made every other dog in the neighborhood join in the barking. The meatballs were waiting in the yard, near the far end of the sidewalk that reached the curb, next to the mailbox, beside the fresno tree, under the bedroom window. He figured the dog would have its snack and walk off before the chemical made it sick. Somebody would find the animal in the alley the next morning. Marcelo told himself that at least he wasn't trespassing onto anyone's property. And if a dog happened to walk into his yard, where it shouldn't have been in the first place but came anyway and ate something that made it sick, was that really his fault? Where did it say his yard was open for dogs to come do their business?

Marcelo listened. The dog wasn't making a sound, but he sensed it was close to the house. He felt as if he'd trained his ears to hear what couldn't be heard, the way some people believed animals had the ability to see spirits that couldn't be seen. He whispered in the dark, "Closer, Charro. Un poquito más, Charro boy." Marcelo fell asleep listening to the distinct sound of dry leaves being stepped on right outside his window.

The next morning he was ready for a new beginning. Olivia made breakfast and he talked about his day while they ate. He had to check on some cattle off Southmost Road, visit an old man who owned a few Shetland ponies and gave rides at the flea market, and, finally, spend a couple of hours patrolling the river in the late afternoon. Before they knew it, it was almost seven o'clock and he'd have to hurry to be on time for his first appointment. Olivia walked him to the door and kissed him good-bye on the cheek. As he stepped onto the porch, his boot slipped forward and he had to hold on to the door so he wouldn't fall. A puddle of red and brown vomit covered the Welcome mat. The dark liquid trailed down the steps and along the sidewalk, until it turned into tiny drops, barely noticeable. Where the driveway ended, Marcelo found an even larger puddle.

He cleaned the mess by himself because Olivia felt sick as soon as she saw the porch. Junior refused to go out through the front when it was time for school. Marcelo acted confused about what might have happened. Flies had already gathered when he turned on the water hose to spray the porch and sidewalk. Except for some pieces of chewed meat that clung to the steps, most of what the animal had left behind flowed down the street and into the gutter. Marcelo tried to hide his guilt, but he couldn't help feeling bad when he saw the specks of blood in the puddle. He told himself he was only doing what he had to, what any workingman would've done. Nobody could blame a man for trying to hold on to his job. It wasn't his fault Sanchez hadn't listened. He had fair warning. Marcelo poured a jug of Clorox on the cement and scrubbed it hard with a tire brush. It took most of a can of Lysol to get rid of the bad smell around the steps. He threw the brush and the Welcome mat into the trash can. When he was driving away, the dog rushed out of Sanchez's yard barking and chasing him halfway down the street, past the red and brown stream and the gutter where it disappeared.

This was the morning Marcelo gave up. He'd get earplugs. They'd move to another neighborhood if they had to. Anything, but he wouldn't try to hurt the dog again. Charro barked on and off for the next few weeks. One night on, one night off. It was getting to where Marcelo could almost guess which nights the dog would come around. He began to accept the barking as part of his life. The noise never lasted more than fifteen or twenty minutes anyway. He used the time to go to the bathroom and relieve himself, instead of waiting until later, when he really had to go. He read the newspaper, which he never had a chance to do during the day. Sometimes he finished the paperwork he handed in every week. Once, he shaved. Another night he trimmed his toenails. He looked forward to his time alone. A couple of nights he even woke up by himself.

He was getting to work on time, especially to his weekly meetings. The supervisor had been going over how the USDA was extending its air surveillance program to the lower Rio

Grande Valley. Marcelo wasn't looking forward to flying in a small plane once a week, but he figured he'd still have a few days to patrol on horseback. The other livestock inspectors were looking forward to a break from the heat. A younger inspector joked around and asked if the plane had an air conditioner. It was after one of these meetings that Olivia called the office. The supervisor answered the phone and said she sounded upset. Marcelo talked to her, but he couldn't get her to calm down. All she could say was that she'd had an accident. The supervisor told Marcelo it'd probably be a good idea if he went ahead and took care of his family. They'd call it a sick day.

Olivia met him in the carport. She was holding Arturo in her arms. The baby smiled and kicked his chubby legs when he saw his father walking toward him.

"I never saw him, Marcelo. I never saw him."

Marcelo noticed a lump of black and reddish brown hair sticking out from underneath the Oldsmobile. It looked as if someone's fur coat had been run over. He walked around to the side and saw blood dripping from the dog's mouth.

"I didn't mean to, Marcelo. Fue un accidente."

"It's okay, Olivia."

"We were late for the doctor's, and Arturo, he wouldn't let me put him in the baby seat."

"He doesn't like to be away from his mama."

"I looked back before I put it in reverse," she said. "But then the car rolled over something and I heard the worst sound, like crying, like I ran over somebody. I thought about the little Gomez boy. He's always running around in the streets. Me puse bien nerviosa. I didn't know what to do, Marcelo. I put it in drive."

"Cacas," the baby said and pointed at the backside of the dog.

This only made Olivia cry more. Marcelo held her in his arms. She was shaking. He helped her inside the house, and the baby stayed with her on the bed.

He walked back outside and squatted next to Charro. At least the body was far enough away from the street that the neighbors couldn't see. He imagined himself having to tell Sanchez what had happened. He wished he hadn't let himself get so mad the last time Sanchez came over. There was no way his neighbor would ever believe that it was Olivia who had been driving and that it was an accident. But what could he do? The dog was dead. Whether it was him or Olivia, nothing was going to bring the animal back to life. It was better if the boy believed the dog had run away again. At least it wouldn't be a shock to him this time.

Marcelo dragged the body farther into the carport and around the left side of the house, where the bougainvilleas blocked anyone from seeing him. Once he was in the backyard, he locked the wooden gate. Next to the cuartito, where he kept the water heater and all his yard tools, looked like a good place to lay the body. He walked back to the carport and used the water hose to spray the last traces of the dog off the concrete and into the grass. Then he pulled a shovel out of the cuartito and started digging a hole.

Marcelo scooped load after load of moist dirt. He tried not to think about what he was doing. The rain from two nights earlier had softened the ground, and he was grateful this made the digging a little easier. At least it wasn't too hot yet. His work would be done in no time, then he'd have the rest of the day free. He could wash the car or change the oil. He could take Olivia out to lunch and get her out of the house.

He stopped digging after a while and sat on the back porch steps. The hole looked deep enough to bury the dog, but something didn't feel right. What he had done to the animal only seemed crueler when he looked at the dead body. He felt that he owed Sanchez and his kid more than just a hole in the ground. He thought about it for a few minutes and decided to build a box for the dog. He looked around the cuartito and under the house, but he didn't have enough wood to make anything the animal would fit in. What he did have was a stack of cardboard boxes that Olivia had saved. He sliced the two largest ones with his buck knife and used some duct tape to hold them together. So the box wouldn't bend in the middle when he lowered it, he placed a piece of plywood on the bottom. He laid the animal on top of some old blankets and its splotched tongue flopped out. After he closed the dog's mouth, he sealed the top of the box with duct tape.

Marcelo hung his work shirt on the porch railing and began digging a larger hole. For the box to fit, he figured the grave needed to be at least five feet long and three feet wide. The sun had come out from behind the clouds and made the

morning hot. Each shovelload felt a little heavier than the
last. His back would hurt later. He had good reasons for
burying the dog in his backyard, but he also knew he could
never stand before Sanchez and his boy and tell them what
had happened. He tried to console himself with the fact that
he had built a box for the dog. It wasn't anything fancy, but
in a small way it helped relieve his guilt. After a while he
stepped into the hole and shoveled the dirt around him. The
last time he'd worked this hard was when his father had
passed away and, in order to save some money, he and his
brothers dug the grave themselves. There were two shovels
and five brothers. They took turns: two brothers working,
two brothers resting in the shade, one brother telling stories
about their father's life. They talked about how their father
had lived on both sides of the river, but he'd always called it
el Río Bravo. He used to say his biggest mistake in life was al-
lowing his sons to be born Americans. He wanted everyone
to know he was puro mexicano and had no desire to change.
Specific instructions had been left for his body to be taken to
the ranchito outside of Matamoros where his parents and his
grandparents were buried. Marcelo thought about how different he was from this man. What would his father have
done about the dog? Right or wrong, he always seemed sure
of what he did. Marcelo had tried to live his father's life, but
now it felt as if he were standing in the middle of a river trying to stretch his arms and touch both sides. No matter what
he did, he'd never reach far enough.

He had been working for a couple of hours when he heard Olivia calling him from the back porch. His undershirt was drenched with sweat and he felt as if he'd been digging all day. Marcelo put down the shovel to find out what she needed, but he couldn't see her over the edge of the grave. He realized then that he'd dug a lot deeper than he needed to.

Don't Believe Anything
He Tells You

Jerry Fuentes

ere's a piece of advice for you: If a guy named Jerry
Fuentes comes knocking at your front door trying to
sell you something, tell him you're not interested and then
lock the door.

Jerry Fuentes is my cousin and he's a salesman. He might
tell you he's something else, use a different word to describe
what he does, but what he is is a salesman. And if you're not
careful, he'll sell you something you had no intention of buying, never needed, and will probably regret for a long time
after he and his cheap cologne have left your house. I know,
because it happened to me.

"Hey, *primo*, how's it going?" he said, standing at my front door one day.

I hate it when he calls me primo. He calls everybody primo, even guys who aren't his cousins or related to him in any way. A few years ago, he moved to San Antonio and was working as a sports promoter. That's what he told the whole family. He had business cards with his beeper number and a slogan that said JERRY FUENTES — YOUR PERSONAL SPORTS PROMOTER. Jerry's got the connections, man, his brother Gabe kept saying. So Anna and I drove up to watch the Spurs play the Bulls, and there was Jerry out in front of the Alamodome, scalping tickets. He set us up all right, but the tickets weren't cheap. Then when we were walking into the building we heard Jerry go, "Hey, *primo*." We turned around and he was talking to a Chinese guy.

That day Jerry came over, he walked into the house and sat right down in my La-Z-Boy. It was probably still warm from me sitting there, flipping through the TV channels. That was the first time Jerry had ever come by, but it looked like he'd been sitting in that chair for years. He looked relaxed, like he owned the place almost. He was wearing a light green sports coat with a pair of slacks that had sharp creases. The top button of his dress shirt was undone and some chest hairs were sticking out.

We didn't see each other in those days, except at weddings and funerals. Not that we saw each other that much when we were growing up. Jerry's ten years older than me, but now that we're both getting older, the difference in our ages doesn't feel that huge. He has more hair than I do and I think he uses hair spray. He's in shape for a guy in his forties, but I'm sure he's never done what you'd call hard work. Either way, staying young has helped him out with the women. I have to hand it to him there. Jerry's never been married and he always has a little movida on the side. Sometimes I wish I had done more of that when I had the chance. But that was part of the trouble at his last job. He was selling frozen steaks, door-to-door, for Archer Meats and spending a little too much time with some of the Valley housewives. Then there was more trouble when the supervisor figured out that Jerry was using the company meat to feed everybody who showed up at his pachangas. Jerry argued with him that each and every one of those steaks was an investment for the company and would, in time, be turned into a profit, which was one of his bigger lies, but it just goes to show you the guy has little or no respect for what's not his. That's why it wasn't any big surprise to see him sitting all comfortable in my chair.

Before Jerry could say anything, I told him I was on my way to pick up Anna, so I only had a few minutes. Really, she wasn't getting off for another hour, but I figured it was probably a good idea to have an excuse in case he was here on business. Anna works at a small accounting office close to the stadium. She does bookkeeping, taxes, and filing for the man who owns the business. Her hours are nine to five, Monday through Friday, except during tax season, when she has to go in on the weekends. She's good with numbers and handles all the money in our house. Payday comes and I hand her the check. I tell her, As long as you don't run off to Las Vegas, I don't care what you do with the money. Not that I'm rich or anything. That isn't going to happen working at the bridge. I've been there eight years so far. As long as there's a bridge to Mexico, I have a job. That's how I like to think about it. Good, dependable work. I think that's what Anna likes the most about me. Especially the "dependable" part. I've thought about applying for the Border Patrol, but Anna thinks it's dangerous work. She likes to tell me that we don't need the money, that we're already rich in other ways. I won the lottery when I married you, she likes to say. Sometimes Anna has a nice way of putting things, but the truth is I haven't been feeling like such a rich guy lately.

I had the late shift at the bridge that night. I'd been home all day, working around the house. I spent some time reading the *Herald* and washed the car about eleven o'clock. After lunch, I took a nap and then watched an *Andy Griffith* rerun. It had been quiet all afternoon until Jerry knocked on my door.

"So what's up, Jerry?" I asked, bracing myself for what might be coming.

He said, "It's about the future. Do you ever think about the future?"

"Yeah, I guess. As much as the next guy."

I wasn't sure what he was getting at, but I knew he didn't

come over to compare horoscopes. He was looking over at a wedding picture sittting on top of the TV set.

"How long you been married now, primo?"

"Almost six years." It was a stupid question to ask me, since he'd been at the wedding and knew damn well how long it had been. He was just trying to soften me up for something.

"Six years?" he said. "It's time to start thinking about having some little Georges, no?"

"Maybe. We haven't really talked about it."

We had talked about it, but it wasn't any of Jerry's business. Anna and I had decided to wait a couple of years. It was a mutual decision, but you could say I encouraged it. What's the rush? I told her.

"That's great, George. You have a beautiful wife." He kept looking at the wedding picture while he was saying this. It was almost as if I wasn't in the room and he was talking to himself. I looked over at the picture and thought Anna did look kind of nice. Sometimes you can overlook these things.

I started remembering the last time I saw Jerry at the bridge. He had pulled up in his red Firebird with this pretty girl who couldn't have been more than twenty, maybe twenty-two at the most. She was young enough to be a student at the college, if that tells you anything. Anyway, Jerry looked drunk, and his right hand was resting between the girl's skinny legs. She was wearing a black miniskirt and a white shirt that I think was see-through, but I couldn't tell for sure, so I won't guarantee you. Her long brown hair came over her shoulders, and she wore a necklace with a gold cross that reached way down into her shirt — probably a lot further down than I should have been looking. She had on maroon lipstick that made her lips look like she was getting ready to kiss you even when she wasn't. Jerry smiled when he saw me staring at his girl a little too long. Then he turned to her and said, Say hello, Monica. The girl giggled, looked up at me, and said, Hello, Monica. Then Jerry laughed and reached into the ashtray to pull out a bunch of change for the toll. Later, primo, he said. His tires screeched a little as he took off. When I counted the coins he was a dime short.

Jerry was now leaning forward in my chair and looking at me. He was quiet for a few seconds. Trying to find inspiration for what he was about to tell me, I guess. His hands were together, and it actually seemed that he might have something honest to say.

"Do you ever think of what might happen to Anna if, God forbid, something were to happen to you?" he finally said.

So now I'm wondering, What the hell does Jerry know that I don't? Is there some disease in our family nobody ever told me about, and now he's here to tell me I have six months to live? And why Jerry? I can think of a dozen other relatives I'd rather hear it from.

"The reason I ask you about the future is that I'm now a pre-arranger for Buena Vista." He reached over and handed me a brochure.

I'd only been to two funerals at Buena Vista. The first time was for my grandmother and the second time for my grandfather. Jerry was there because they were his grandmother and grandfather, too. Both times the long procession bounced its way along the bumpy road in front of the project homes and then turned into the cemetery before it got to Highway 77. My grandparents died a few years ago, but listening to Jerry tell me he was a "pre-arranger," I started getting the same heavy feeling in my chest I had when they lowered the caskets. I sat back and opened the brochure, except I'm not sure why. The thought of death is not something I'm comfortable with. It never has been. I only went to those funerals because my family wouldn't have let me live it down if I hadn't gone. And when I think about it, the only reason I even let Jerry in the house and didn't throw him out was the fact that he was family.

"Jerry, I'm only thirty-three," I said after a while. "I think I have some time before I have to think about these kinds of things."

"That's what you would think," he said. "That's what everybody thinks."

He was shaking his head. I could tell he was disappointed with me.

"Remember Pete Hernandez? You think the cancer thought *he* was too young? And what about that twenty-six-year-old guy in the paper yesterday? Poor guy hit his head in the shower and woke up dead in the morning, next to his wife."

"Yeah, but . . ."

"Nobody likes to think about these things, primo. Aren't you the kind of husband that would want Anna taken care of in a time like this?" He was saying it with his head tilted to the right. His hair was sitting perfectly still, even with the ceiling fan on high.

"Sure."

What else was I going to say? *No*, I don't want her taken care of? I knew that was one of Jerry's salesman questions, where the customer didn't have a choice but to agree with him. These questions of his always made me feel dumb, which was just one more reason to hate the guy.

"I know what you're thinking, primo. You're thinking that this is going to be expensive."

It wasn't anything like what I was thinking, but I let him go on. My mind was on the idea of Anna dying and me being alive. When my grandmother died, she left my grandfather behind. They'd been married sixty-five years. About a month after they buried her, my grandfather drove his truck fifty miles an hour, head-on, into a palm tree and was dead long before the ambulance showed up. I always thought he did it on purpose, so he could be with my grandmother. I considered it true love. And as much as I cared for Anna, I didn't know if I could do the same for her.

"Well, that's why I'm here," Jerry said. "I came up with a plan to make it affordable for you. It has to do with both you and Anna buying the services and burial space, side by side. That way I know I can get you a discount." He said it like I should be thanking him already, maybe pulling out my checkbook and signing up right there and then.

"The other thing is, you don't have to pay for it all right now. I can set you up on a five-year plan, ten-year, whatever. It's just like buying a house. You pay off a little every month until, before you know it, it's all taken care of."

But it wasn't anything like buying a house. I'd be dead.

And there'd be no kitchen, no bedroom, no bathroom, no driveway, no garage, no yard. Nothing. Just a coffin and a lot of dirt all around me is what there'd be.

"This way you won't have to worry later. N'hombre, primo, believe me, you don't want to be thinking about these sorts of things if, God forbid, Anna happens to pass before you do." He crossed himself as he said this. It seemed like the idea of Anna dying before me was sadder to him.

I opened the brochure again and looked at the different models of coffins. Some of the fancier ones had a nice shine to them like a polished-up lowrider. The cheaper ones were made of a dark wood and didn't look so comfortable. They also didn't look like they would last as long as the polished ones. I wondered which one Anna would pick out for me, if it were her decision and not mine. She'd probably go with something middle-of-the-road. Not too expensive, not too cheap. But dependable. It had to be dependable. Then I thought about the one suit I owned and how I'd worn it to every family wedding for the past few years. Is that really how I wanted everybody to see me for the last time? Not that any of these things would matter in the end, but it did get me thinking.

"*Primo,* I don't want you to say a word. I want you to talk about it with your beautiful wife, and then tell me what you've decided. Remember, I can make this plan work for you."

We stood up at the same time, and he opened his arms to give me an abrazo. He held me tight for a few seconds, patting me on the back over and over again. I felt like I was at a funeral for somebody who had died young and unexpectedly.

If it hadn't been for Anna, that would've been the end of all the pre-arrangement talk.

"Jerry called," she said. She woke up to tell me this. I had come home from work and we were lying in bed with the lights off. "He told me how you were interested in making the pre-arrangements. He said he wanted to know how I felt about it and if there were any questions he could help me with."

"I never said I was interested."

"That's not what he said. And anyway, it sounds like a good idea."

Anna never saw the problems in Jerry that I did. She thought he meant well, and all he needed was a wife who understood him and could straighten him out. Once, she even tried to set Jerry up with one of her single girlfriends. Like he needed help finding a date.

"What's a good idea?" I said.

"Being prepared, it's a good idea. You know what happened to my mother."

I knew what happened with her mother — I just never understood it. One day she was fine, the next day she had cancer. The doctors couldn't do anything for her. It happened that quick. And because she had never made "arrangements," she ended up being buried on the other side of the cemetery from where Anna's father was buried. It meant something to Anna that they be together, side by side. I never understood what the big deal was. I didn't see the point of being in the ground dead next to someone else who was dead. To me, dead was dead.

"Don't you want to be together . . . you know, when it's that time?" Anna turned to look at me.

Hearing her question made me think of Jerry's questions. I started feeling that she might have picked it up from his phone call, or maybe he'd coached her on what to say to me, to get me to say yes.

"Listen, to start with, Jerry made that up. I'm not interested. He's just trying to get his commission, and he's using us to get it. Don't believe him. Don't believe anything he tells you."

Anna was quiet for a few seconds, and then she moved a little closer. "He told me you might say that, but it was only because you're afraid of dying and losing me."

She put her head on my chest, and a minute later she fell asleep.

For the next week, I didn't answer the phone because I thought it might be Jerry. He left at least two messages on the machine every day.

"Hey, *primo,* I don't remember if I left my business card with you," he said, even though we both knew he had, "but let me give you my office number and my pager, just in case. Ready?"

Or, "Hey, *primo,* it's me, Jerry. Just checking to see if you had any more questions. I know I can make this work for you. We're family, remember."

I never picked up the phone or called him back, but it didn't matter, because Anna did. She was getting more and more excited about the whole thing. One day she even went to the Buena Vista offices and looked at the coffins in person. She said she'd already picked out two of them for us, and they matched. I told her it wouldn't matter unless we were hit by the same bus and died together. Anna said she didn't know why I was being so negative. She said that she'd talked to Olga, a woman who worked in the office next to her, and that Olga and her husband had already made pre-arrangements.

"Yeah," I said, "But Olga is around sixty years old, and her husband is about eighty and has a hole in his throat from smoking since he was a kid. That makes sense. You pre-arrange when you're eighty and you have a hole in your throat, not when you're thirty-three and healthy like we are. This is crazy. I can't believe you're listening to these crazy people and my psycho cousin."

It was that, the part about being crazy, that brought the tears rolling down her cheeks. She threw herself on the bed, facedown with a pillow over her head, and didn't get up for the rest of the night. And from there, as they say, it was a done deal.

Jerry brought over the papers for us to sign the next morning. He was all smiles. You would have thought we'd just bought a brand-new Cadillac from him. There were places on the contract where I signed my full name and others where I only put my initials. The papers said we were to pay $115 a month until everything was paid off in ten years. Jerry pointed out how we were actually saving money by making the arrangements now instead of in the future, when they'd for sure be more expensive.

"¿Qué te dije, primo? Didn't I tell you I'd take care of you?"

I just looked over at Anna. She could tell I was upset with the way things had turned out. She smiled at me the way she had at our wedding. It wasn't exactly a happy smile, but more like a smile that said everything was good in her world. She had a roof over her head, clothes on her back, food in the refrigerator, a nice car to drive, and now a pair of pre-arranged funerals. She reached out and gave my hand a tight squeeze.

"I think George is a little nervous about the contract," she said. Her hair was pulled into a bun and it made her look older. She looked like somebody's mother.

"Primo, you know what I'm going to do?" He clicked his ballpoint pen and put it back in his sports coat. "I'm not going to cash this first check or hand in the paperwork. I'll give you until tomorrow to think about it. And if you're still not sure, I'll tear everything up and give you back your check. How about that?"

I knew this was another one of Jerry's salesman techniques, and if I agreed to it, I'd probably end up buying another casket somehow in the deal. But I went and took him up on his offer, just to make him sweat it out an extra day.

That night when I left work, I did something I hadn't done in years. I stopped by the Jiffy-Mart and bought a six-pack of Budweiser. Then I got back in the car and drove around for the next few hours. The way I saw it, there were decisions you made over a hot cup of coffee and there were decisions you made over a cold beer. This was the cold-beer kind of decision.

The first place I drove by was Lincoln Park. Some kids were hanging out by the entrance, smoking cigarettes. I thought about being that old and sneaking out of the house to do the same exact thing. It felt good to be older now and have nothing to do but drink a few beers. I didn't need to ask anybody's permission, either. It was my car, and I was drinking the beer I bought with my own money. I even slid a Van Halen cassette into the tape player. By the time I was back on International, I'd finished my first beer and thrown it in the backseat. I popped open another one and held it between my legs, just cruising.

I was driving on Boca Chica when I saw Jerry's red Firebird going the other way. I made a U-turn. I wanted to stop him and ask what the hell he thought he was doing pulling a fast one on Anna and me. We now owed over $13,000 in pre-arrangements I never wanted and neither would've Anna if he hadn't kept bugging us. I still couldn't believe she had made me sign those papers. The Firebird pulled over into a parking lot. Through his back window, I could see a girl in the passenger seat. They were kissing, and Jerry was running his hands through her hair. Then he kissed her on the neck, and his head kept going lower and lower, until I couldn't see him anymore. I wondered if she was the same girl with the lips and the gold cross hanging so far down into her shirt, Monica. As I drove away, I imagined him kissing the cross. I felt like going by Jerry's house and throwing the empties in his yard.

I had one beer left when I drove by Buena Vista. The moon was full and I could see far into the cemetery. It looked like a city park without any swings or slides. I left the car in an empty lot across the street. The chain-link fence around Buena Vista was six feet high, but it looked taller at 1:30 in the morning. I was carrying my last beer in the plastic ring holder it came in. I hung the beer can on the fence and climbed over as soon as there were no cars passing by.

I walked around, drinking, looking at all the names on the tombstones. Garcia, Paredes, Ramirez, Martinez, Saldaña, Lucio, Zuniga. When I found my grandmother's grave, I got down on my knees and prayed a Hail Mary and told her that I knew she was in heaven and I missed her. Then I looked for my grandfather's grave and ended up walking around for over an hour and still not finding it. I'll admit I was a little drunk, but I wasn't so pedo that I couldn't read a tombstone. I must have looked at three hundred of them. I finally rested in a clear space on the grass. The air was still warm, but the grass felt cool. It was peaceful lying there. I looked up at the moon and watched the clouds pass by. I wanted to figure out what to do about Jerry, but all I kept thinking about was my grandfather. I could see him stepping on the accelerator, unbuckling himself from the seat belt, heading for a palm tree that was getting closer every second, wanting nothing more than to be with my grandmother. And at least there in the cemetery, he never even got near her. What was so wrong with being alone? I wanted to tell him that it wasn't that bad. I liked spending my days at the house. I liked it when tax season rolled around and Anna worked weekends. I liked driving home alone at night after work, sometimes taking the long way. And if I had the chance, I'd probably go out drinking more often, maybe even start smoking again. Then I thought about when we were getting married and I said, "I do," when the priest asked, "Until death do you part?" I thought about how I had always been willing to live up to that and more. And I probably would have kept doing so happily if it hadn't been for my cousin.

It was 2:50 in the morning by the time I made it home. Anna was sound asleep. The flush of the toilet or me kicking off my shoes didn't bother her any. She just grabbed more blanket and rolled over on her side. There was a note sitting next to the alarm clock. It said, Jerry called and he wants you to call him back. Love, Anna. I crawled into bed and tried to fall asleep. I looked over at Anna and she was lying on her back now. I was on my back, too. There we were, side by side. She was facing the ceiling and her body was very still. I kept looking at her, just to make sure she was breathing.

Yolanda

When I can't sleep at night I think of Yolanda Castro. She was a woman who lived next door to us one summer when I was growing up. I've never told Maggie about her because it's not something she'd appreciate knowing. Trust me. Tonight, like most nights, she fell asleep before I was even done brushing my teeth. And now all I can hear are little snores. Sometimes she even talks to herself, shouts out other people's names, and then in the morning says she can't remember any of it. Either way, I let her go on sleeping. She's over on her side of the bed. It's right where she ought to be. This thing with Yolanda doesn't really concern her.

I was only twelve years old when Frank and Yolanda Castro moved into the beige house with green trim. Frank pulled up on our street in a U-Haul he'd driven all the way from California to Texas. I remember it being a different neighborhood back then. Everybody knew everybody, and people left their doors unlocked at night. You didn't worry about people stealing shit you didn't lock up. I'm talking about more than twenty years ago now. I'm talking about before some drunk spent all afternoon in one of the cantinas on Fourteenth Street, then drove his car straight into the Rivas front yard and ran over the Baby Jesus that was still lying in the manger because Lonny Rivas was too flojo to put it away a month after Christmas, and then the guy tried to run, but fell down, asleep, in our yard, and when the cops were handcuffing him all he could say was *ma-ri-juan-a,* which even then, at the age of fifteen, I knew wasn't a good thing to say when you were being arrested. This was before Pete Zuniga was riding his brand-new ten-speed from Western Auto and, next to the Friendship Garden, saw a white dude who'd been knifed a couple of dozen times and was floating in the green water of the resaca. Before some crazy woman hired a curandera to put a spell on her daughter's ex-boyfriend, which really meant hiring a couple of hit men from Matamoros to do a drive-by. Before the cops ever had to show up at El Disco de Oro Tortillería. Like holding up a 7-Eleven was getting old, right? You know, when you could sit at the Brownsville Coffee Shop #1 and not worry about getting it in the back while you ate your menudo. When you didn't have to put an alarm *and* the Club on your car so it wouldn't end up in Reynosa. Before my father had to put iron bars on the windows and doors because some future convict from the junior high was always breaking into the house. And before my father had to put a fence in the front because, in his words, I'm sick and tired of all those damn dogs making poo in my yard. I guess what I'm trying to say is, things were different back then.

Frank Castro was an older man, in his fifties by that point, and Yolanda couldn't have been more than thirty, if that. My mother got along with Yolanda okay and even helped her get a job at the HEB store where she had worked since before I was born. You could say that was where the problems started, because Frank Castro didn't want his wife working at HEB, or any other place for that matter. You have no business being in that grocery store, I heard him yell one night when I was trying to fall asleep. I could hear almost everything Frank yelled that summer. Our houses were only a few yards apart, and my window was the closest to the action. My father's bougainvilleas were the dividing line between the two properties. I heard Yolanda beg Frank to please let her take the job. I heard Frank yell something in Spanish about how no woman in his family had ever worked behind a cosmetics counter, selling lipstick. I heard her promise she'd only work part-time, and she'd quit if they ever scheduled her on nights or weekends. I heard her tell him how much she loved him and how she'd never take a job that would keep them apart. Francisco, tú eres mi vida, she said to him. I heard him get real quiet. Then I heard Frank and Yolanda Castro making love. I didn't know what making love sounded like back then, but I can tell you now that's what it was.

If you saw what Yolanda looked like, you might not have blamed Frank for not wanting her to leave the house. It also wouldn't have been a big mystery to you how she went into the store applying for a job in the meat department and ended up getting one in cosmetics. The only girl I'd ever seen that even came close to being as beautiful as Yolanda was in a *Playboy* I found under my parents' bed the summer before. The girl in the magazine had the same long black hair, light brown skin, and green eyes that Yolanda did, only she was sitting bareback on an Appaloosa.

The thing I remember most about Frank was his huge forearms. They were like Popeye's, except with a lot more black and gray hair mixed in. But the hair on his arms was just the beginning. There wasn't a time I saw the guy that he didn't look like he could've used a good shave. And it didn't help that his thick eyebrows were connected into one long eyebrow that stretched across the bottom of his forehead like a piece of electrical tape. He was average size, but he looked short and squatty when he stood next to Yolanda. Frank was a mechanic at the airport and, according to my father, probably made good money. I was with my father the first time he met Frank. He always made it a point to meet any new neighbors and then come back to the house and give a full report to my mother, who would later meet the neighbors herself and say he was exaggerating about how shifty so-and-so's eyes were or how rich he thought another neighbor might be because he had one of those new foreign cars in the driveway, un carro extranjero, a Toyota or a Honda. Frank was beginning to mow his front yard when we walked up. My father introduced me as his boy, and I shook our neighbor's sweaty hand. I've lived thirty-six years on this earth and never shaken hands with a bear, but I have a good idea that it wouldn't be much different from shaking Frank Castro's hand. Even his fingers needed a haircut. Frank stood there answering a couple of my father's questions about whether he liked the neighborhood (he liked it) and how long he had lived in California before moving back to Texas (ten years — he held up both hands to show us exactly how many). Suddenly, my father nodded and said we had to go. He turned around and walked off, then looked over his shoulder and yelled at me to hurry up. This whole time, Frank had not shut off his mower. My father was forced to stand there and shout over the sound of the engine. The report on Frank wasn't pretty when we got back to the house. From that point on, my father would only refer to him as El Burro.

It wasn't just my father. Nobody liked Frank. He had this thing about his yard where he didn't want anybody getting near it. We found this out one day when Lonny and I were throwing the football around in the street. Lonny was showing off and he threw the ball over my head, way over, and it landed in Frank's yard. When I was getting the ball, Frank opened the front door and yelled something about it being private property. Then he went over, turned on the hose, and started watering his yard and half the street in front of his yard. He did this every afternoon from that day on. The hose with a spray gun in his right hand, and a Schlitz tallboy in his left. Lonny thought we should steal the hose when Frank wasn't home, or maybe poke a few holes in it, just to teach the fucker a lesson. One Saturday morning we even saw him turn the hose on some Jehovahs who were walking up the street towards his house. A skinny man wearing a tie and short-sleeve shirt kept trying to give him a pamphlet, but Frank wasn't listening.

My mother gave Yolanda a ride to work every day. In the afternoons, Yolanda got off work early enough to be waiting for Frank to pull up in his car and drive her back to the house. My mother told us at home that Yolanda had asked Frank to teach her how to drive when they first got married but that Frank had said she was his princesa now and any place she needed to go, he'd take her. One morning, when both my mother and Yolanda had the day off, my mother asked her if she wanted to learn how to drive. They drove out by the port, and my mother pulled over so Yolanda could take the wheel. I was hanging out at the Jiffy-Mart, down the street, when I saw Yolanda driving my mother's car. Yolanda honked the horn, and they both waved at me as they turned the corner.

That night — like a lot of nights that summer — I listened to Frank and Yolanda Castro. What they said went something like this:

"I can show you."

"I don't wanna see."

"Why not?"

"Because you have *no* business driving a car around town."

"But this way you don't have to pick me up every day. You can come straight home, and I'll be here already, waiting."

"I don't care. I'm talking about you learning to drive."

"Frank, it's nothing."

"You don't even have a car. What do you want with a license?"

"I can buy one."

"With what?"

"I've been getting bonuses. The companies give us a little extra if we sell more of their makeup."

"Is that right?"

"It isn't that much, Frank."

"And then?"

"Well, maybe I can buy a used one."

"It's because of that store."

"What's wrong with the store?"

"It's putting ideas in your head."

"Frank, what ideas?"

"Ideas! Is there some place I haven't taken you?"

"No."

"Well, then?"

"Francisco."

"Don't 'Francisco' me."

"Baby . . ."

"¡Qué no!"

They were beginning to remind me of one of my mother's novelas, which she was probably watching in the living room at that very moment. Things like that usually made me want to laugh — and I did a little, into my pillow, but it was only because I couldn't believe I was actually hearing it, and I could see Frank Castro pounding me into the ground with his big forearms if he ever found out.

"No! I said."

"I'm not Trini."

"I never said . . ."

"Then stop treating me like her. ¿No sabes qué tanto te quiero, Francisco?"

It got quiet for a while after that. Then there was the sound of something hitting the floor, the sound of two bodies dropping on a bed with springs that had seen better days (and nights), the sound of Yolanda saying, *Ay, Diosito,* over and over and over again — just like my tía Hilda did the day her son, my cousin Rudy, almost drowned in the swimming pool at the Civic Center — then the sound of the bed springs making their own crazy music, and the sound of what I imagine a bear is like when he's trying to make little bears.

Yolanda kept getting a ride to work with my mother, and Frank kept bringing her home in the afternoons. My mother had offered to drive Yolanda to the DPS office and let her borrow our car for the driving part of the test, but Yolanda said she'd changed her mind and didn't want to talk about it. I heard my mother telling my father what she'd said, and they agreed it probably had something to do with Frank. El Burro, my father let out when they didn't have anything else to say.

It was the Fourth of July when I got sick that summer. I remember my mother wouldn't let me go outside with Lonny. He kept yelling at me from the street that night to stop being a baby and come out of the house so I could pop some firecrackers. We'd been talking all week about shooting some bottle rockets in the direction of Frank's house. It didn't feel like anything at first, just a fever, but the next morning we knew it was the chicken pox. My mother had to miss a few days of work, staying home with me until I got over the worst part. After that, Yolanda volunteered to come look in on me when she wasn't working. But I told my mother I didn't want her coming over when I still looked like those dead people in that *Night of the Living Dead* movie. My mother said Yolanda would understand I was sick, and if she didn't, that's what I'd get for watching those kinds of movies. So for about a week she came over in the mornings and we watched *The Price Is Right* together. Yolanda was great at guessing the prices of things, and she said it was from working in a grocery store and having a good memory. I told her I thought she should go on the show. She laughed and said she probably wouldn't win anything, since she'd be too nervous. What I meant to say was that she should go on the show and be one of the girls who stands next to the car, smiling. She was prettier than any of them, but I never told her that, because I got embarrassed whenever I thought about saying it.

If Yolanda came over in the afternoon, we'd watch *General Hospital* together. She said she'd been watching it for years. There wasn't anything else on at that hour, so I didn't really care. Once, she brought over some lime sherbert, and we played Chinese checkers in my room until she had to get home to Frank Castro. Each time she left she'd reach down and give me a little kiss on the cheek, and each time her hair smelled like a different fruit. Sometimes like a pear, sometimes like a strawberry, sometimes like an apple. The strawberry was my favorite.

This was about the time when Frank said that from now on, he would take Yolanda to work in the morning — no matter how out of the way it was for him, or the fact that he and my mother were always pulling out of the driveway at the same time. A week or two went by, and then my mother told my father that Frank had started showing up at the store in the middle of the day, usually during his lunch hour, but sometimes also at two or three in the afternoon. He wouldn't talk to Yolanda, but instead just hung out by the magazine rack, pretending to read a wrestling magazine. Yolanda tried to ignore him. My mother said she had talked to her in the break room, but Yolanda kept saying it was nothing, that Frank's hours had changed at the airport.

There was one Saturday when he was off from work, and as usual, he spent it in his front yard, sitting in a green lawn chair, drinking tallboys. He had turned on the sprinkler and was watching his grass and half the street get a good watering. Lonny and I were throwing the football around. Frank sat in that stupid chair all afternoon. He only went in to grab another beer and, I guess, take a piss. Each time he got up and turned around, we shot him the finger.

That night, I heard Frank's voice loud and clear. He wanted answers. Something about a phone number. Something about a customer he'd seen Yolanda talking to a couple of days earlier. Did she think he was blind? What the hell was so funny when the two of them were talking? How many times? he wanted to know. ¡Desgraciado! Where? Goddammit! he wanted to know. What game show? ¡El sanavabiche! Something shattered against the wall and then a few seconds later Yolanda screamed. I sat up. I didn't know if I could form words if I had to. What the hell were you doing listening anyway? they would ask me. There was another scream and then the sound of the back door slamming. I looked out my window and saw Frank Castro chase Yolanda into their backyard. She was wearing a nightgown that came down to her knees. Frank had on the same khakis and muscle shirt he'd worn that afternoon. He only ran a few feet down from the back steps before his head hit the clothesline, and he fell to the ground, hard. Yolanda didn't turn to look back and ran around the right side of their house. I thought she'd gone back inside to call the police. Then I heard footsteps and a tapping on my window. It was Yolanda whispering, Open it, open it.

I didn't say anything for a long time. Yolanda had climbed in and let down the blinds. We were lying on the bed, facing the window. She was behind me, holding me tight. I finally asked her if she wanted a glass of water or some Kool-Aid. I made it myself, I told her. It's the orange kind, I said. I didn't know what else to talk about. She said no, and then she told me to be quiet. I kept thinking, This has to be a dream and any minute now my mother's going to walk in and tell me the barbacoa is sitting on the table and to come eat because we're going to eleven o'clock mass and don't even think about putting on those blue jeans with the patches in the knees ¿me entiendes? But that wasn't happening, and something told me then that no matter what happened after tonight, this was something I'd never forget. There would always be a time *before* Yolanda crawled into my bed and a time *after*. As she held me, I could feel her heart beating. Then I felt her chiches pressed against my back. And even though I couldn't see them, I knew they were perfect like the rest of her. I knew that they'd fit right in the palms of my hands, if only I had enough guts to turn around. Just turn around, that's all I had to do. I thought back to when she was tapping on the window, and I was sure she wasn't wearing a bra. I was sure there was nothing but Yolanda underneath her nightgown. I could have sworn I'd seen even more. I'd been close to a woman's body before. But this wasn't like when my tía Gloria came into town and couldn't believe how much I'd grown, and then she squeezed me so hard my head got lost in her huge and heavily perfumed chiches. And it wasn't anything like the Sears catalog where the girls had a tiny rose at the top of their panties. No, this was Yolanda and she was in my bed, pressed up against my back, like it was the only place in the world for us to be.

I could go on and tell you the rest of the details — how I never turned around and always regretted it, how we stayed there and listened to Frank crying in his backyard, how

Lonny's dad finally called the cops on his ass, how Yolanda had a cousin pick her up the next morning, how she ended up leaving Frank for a man who worked for one of the shampoo companies, how it didn't matter because she'd also been seeing an assistant manager and would be having his baby soon enough, and how it really didn't matter because the assistant manager was already married and wasn't about to leave his wife and kids, and how, actually, none of it mattered because she'd been taking money out of the register and was about to be caught — but that's not the part of the story I like to remember.

In that bed of mine, the one with the Dallas Cowboy pillows and covers, Yolanda and I were safe. We were safe from Frank Castro and safe from anybody else that might try to hurt us. And it was safe for me to fall asleep in Yolanda's arms, with her warm, beautiful body pressed against mine, and dream that we were riding off to some faraway place on an Appaloosa.

Mrs. Perez

Her name was engraved in black cursive letters an inch above the finger holes: *Lola*. The ball's cherry red color and gold swirls made it look as if it were catching fire when she released it down the lane. People stopped to watch when she was up. First, she tugged on her wrist brace to make it snug. Then she dried her fingers over the air vent before she lifted the ball from the tray. Once she was on the floor, she stood absolutely still, her gaze locked on the pins. She was in no hurry. Approaching the foul line, her stride became more fluid as she bent her right knee slightly and trailed her left leg around the back with the grace of a young bride dancing with her new husband for the first time. The ball spun toward the left edge of the lane, held its position, flirted with the gutter, then hooked sharply to the right, exploding into the pocket between the number one and two pins. The destruction echoed through the bowling alley. Her compact size was the source of her power. She measured five feet two inches and weighed 164 pounds, most of it concentrated in her thighs and hips. The ball weighed fifteen pounds. While other sixty-eight-year-olds were slowing down, her body seemed to recover lost years each time she lined her feet up with the dots on the floor. Her living room was a testament to her God-given talent. Every space on the coffee table, windowsill, bookcase, and television held a trophy: Brownsville Ladies' Invitational, First Place; Rio Grande Valley Open, Most Valuable Player; Alamo City Ladies' Classic, Second Place; Bluebonnet Queens Tournament, First Place; Chicago Queen Pins Invitational, First Place; Las Vegas Women's Senior National Championship, Honorable Mention. But this was before the cherry red ball was stolen.

Lola had been at the beauty parlor that afternoon. The girl at the parlor gave her hair an auburn tint that came close to matching its original color. Her hair held a perfectly round shape that rose a few inches and flourished in a curl just above her eyebrows. Women's league play was starting that night and she wanted to look nice. She drove home and couldn't help occasionally catching a glimpse of her hair in the rearview mirror. When she unlocked the front door, she thought she heard a noise, maybe footsteps. She had lived alone for the past sixteen years and had grown used to a quiet house. She put down her purse and listened, but the house was silent. And then right in front of her, somebody ran through the kitchen and out the back door. It happened so fast, she thought she'd imagined it, but there was no imagining the loud slap of the screen door. On the back steps, she saw a teenage boy toss her bowling bag over the chain-link fence and then jump it himself.

"¡Párate! ¡Güerco méndigo! ¡Desgraciado! Somebody stop him! Somebody!" But no one did, and the teenager had enough time to stop in the alley and laugh at the way the old lady was screaming. He was tall and wiry, nothing but skin and bones and a crew cut. His baggy jeans hung extra low on his nalgas. Holding Lola's bowling bag in his right hand, the teenager sauntered away as if he'd just been paged that his lane was ready.

Lola was still in shock when she called the police. She had to look at an old utility bill lying next to the recliner so she could remember her own address. After she hung up the phone, she went back to the kitchen. Off in a corner she found two banana peels on her linoleum floor. Then she noticed the back screen window was ripped open. She blamed herself for not having checked to make sure the windows were down. Not locking your windows was an invitation for somebody to rob you. In the bathroom, the toilet seat was up and the commode was full of bright yellow urine. It would be her luck to get a thief without the decency to flush. She couldn't believe the bedroom when she saw it. The dresser drawers were turned over and the contents were spilled onto the floor in one huge pile. Her underwear and brassieres were mixed in with toenail clippers and costume jewelry. Shoe boxes containing her important documents were emptied on top of this. Old photos that had been stored in a hatbox were scattered in a separate pile. The mattress was turned over and leaning against the wall, as if anyone were idiota enough to still leave her money under a mattress. The only things missing from the bedroom were an old pocket watch that didn't work and had belonged to her late husband, Agustin Perez, and her wedding rings, which she hardly wore anymore. It could've been worse. She made it a point not to keep any money in the house for this very reason. Lola sat in the living room and waited for the police. She thanked God the teenager hadn't touched her trophies. The twenty-three frozen lady bowlers had witnessed the break-in, but they were all in their usual positions. The only thing that was different about the room was the empty spot where she kept her bowling bag.

Her daughter Margie would have something to say about all this. She had been trying to get Lola to sell the small three-bedroom house and live with her in Houston. Her two other daughters were in agreement, but it was Margie who would use the robbery to build her case. Eventually, Lola would have to tell her to mind her own business. She'd lived too long to be talked to like a young girl. Nobody told her what to do or how to live anymore, not a daughter who lived more than

three hundred miles away and not some cabrón who left banana peels on her floor.

She was surprised to see such a young police officer
knocking on her door. He was maybe twenty-five and a little
taller than she was. Her first thought was that she'd been
robbed by a teenage boy and now she was reporting the
crime to his slightly older brother. The officer walked through
the house, letting out a little whistle each time he noticed
more evidence of the break-in. She wished they would have
sent someone with more experience.

"How long have you been a policeman?" she asked.

"Two years, ma'am. Why?"

"Because I asked them to send Timo Hinojosa, he was my
husband's friend. He lives on this street."

"I don't know, but I think Sergeant Hinojosa is getting
ready to retire. He stays at the station a lot, you know. He's
not so young anymore."

"¿Y eso qué quiere decir?"

"I'm sorry, Mrs. Perez. I was just saying that after so
many years, he deserves to not work so hard."

Lola stopped to think about that. She had never seen her
neighbor as an old man, especially since he was a few years
younger than she was.

They sat at the kitchen table so the officer could fill out his
report.

"I saw him with my own eyes," she said.

"Did he look like he was in junior high or high school?"
the officer asked. "Like a teenager?"

"How did you know?"

"The bananas," he said. "Sometimes these kids break in and they spend all their time eating or drinking people's beer. We got a call one time from a woman whose house had been broken into. She wasn't going to call us, but then she found one of these boys in the backyard throwing up."

He started to laugh at this, but stopped when he saw that Lola wasn't smiling.

"It's good he ran off, Mrs. Perez. Some of them get crazy on spray paint and they think they can do anything."

Lola shook her head.

"Can you tell me exactly what he took, ma'am?"

"My bowling ball."

"What else?"

"My bag."

"Your purse?"

"No, my bowling bag, with my ball."

"Anything else?"

"That's not enough for you?"

She explained that it was a polyurethane ball that had cost $175, plus an extra $15 for the fitting, $10 for the engraving, and $30 for a black leather bag that had her full name embroidered on the outside. Her shoes were in the bag and they were worth another $35. Then she remembered her wrist brace, which was another $10. The officer wrote it all down, but he didn't offer much hope. They'd put the word out at the pawnshops. You never know, he said as he was leaving. In all the confusion, Lola forgot to mention the rings or the busted watch.

She sat in the recliner again and looked at her trophies. Most of them had been won with her cherry red ball, and she tried to remember a time before she had the ball. She had started bowling only after her husband died of a bad heart at the age of fifty-two. All the Perez men had heart problems that were only made worse with their tempers. Lola had to admit that in spite of his faults, Agustin had worked hard and had taken care of his family. The girls had been able to go away to college with the savings he had set aside. Lola lived comfortably now because of how tight he was with money throughout their marriage. Over the years, she and Agustin passed by the bowling alley hundreds of times, but they never entered the building. "Puros vicios, that's all you're going to find inside those four walls. People throwing their money away. Parrandeando." Agustin worked as an electrician for the city and earned a decent living, but he never wanted to spend more than absolutely necessary. He considered anything other than work and church to be a waste of time and money, something invented to make sure the workingman stayed poor.

After the girls started school, Lola found a job as a receptionist at a doctor's office. She worked only until two in the afternoon so she could be home when her girls got out of school. The office was an escape from her life of cooking and cleaning. She learned about illnesses she'd never heard of, talked to the patients and the medical representatives who came by, and even helped out the nurses when they were busy. She admired a nurse named Vangie who had gone to school while she was raising her children. Lola and Vangie were about the same age, but Vangie looked much younger in her crisp white uniform. If there weren't too many patients, they would sometimes take their breaks together, either in the file room or behind the office, where Vangie could smoke. Except for some María Félix movies, Lola had never seen a woman smoke so freely.

"You should've been a nurse," Vangie told her one day. She was lighting a cigarette next to the back door.

"It's too late now," Lola said.

"Not really. You could get your nurse's aid certificate."

"I don't have time."

"Sure you do," Vangie said. "It takes less than a year. The doctor might even help you pay for it."

"I don't know, Vangie."

"Well, I think you should." She took a short draw on her cigarette and blew the smoke straight up. "I think you would make a good nurse."

The possibility of a different life surprised Lola. After her first baby, she had never really considered doing anything other than raising her family. She had been a good student in high school and her teachers were always encouraging her to do something with her future. Maybe this was it. The girls were old enough to help around the house and give her time to study. She spent months thinking it over. Then one day Agustin came home from work with the flu. The next morning she brought him into the doctor's office. The waiting room was already crammed with other patients, many of them also suffering through the flu. Agustin became impatient the longer it took. Lola helped the nurses as much as she could, especially when it came Agustin's turn to see the doctor. She couldn't believe how fate had worked to grant her this moment with her husband. Agustin would be able to see how much she'd learned and how easily it came to her. Studying to be a nurse's assistant would be the most natural thing for her to do. She weighed him, took his temperature, read his blood pressure, and handed him the glass bottle for his urine sample. She was methodical in how she did it because she wanted to impress him, although she questioned whether he was well enough to notice anything she was doing. A few days passed before he started feeling better.

"We need to talk," he told her that night.

"¿De qué?"

"About what you do at the doctor's office."

"Did you see all I learned how to do?"

"I saw it. You do this with everybody who comes in?"

"Only when they get busy and they need me."

"And to the men?"

"Sometimes. I don't choose the patients. They just say, 'Mrs. Perez, we need you here, Mrs. Perez, we need you over there.'"

"It don't matter what they say. I don't want you doing that anymore."

"But why?"

"Because I don't want my wife walking around with bottles of you know what."

"It's called a urine sample."

"It's called meados where I come from."

"Ay, you're being crazy now."

"Some man sticks it in that glass bottle, makes his chorro, and then my wife walks around the office like she's carrying a glass of lemonade. And you think I'm the crazy one?"

"Agustin, por favor."

"No, Lola, you're going to stop all of that ahorita mero."

"I can't stop my job."

"Yes, you can. You just tell them tomorrow morning that you're not going to touch any more bottles with meados. If they don't like it, tell them I said to call your husband. I'll explain it to them real clear."

She never told them anything and instead quit at the end of the week. When Vangie asked her why, she said her family needed her.

After she stopped working at the office, Lola saw Vangie only when she or one of her girls was sick. She always stayed a little longer at the office on those visits. Vangie would invite her out to lunch or coffee, and Lola would say she'd call one of these days, but then she never would. Lola might not have seen her again if Vangie hadn't come to offer her condolences at Agustin's Rosary. When Lola looked up from her pew, she realized that the woman standing in front of her was the last friend she could remember having made in more than ten years. They held each other and Lola cried on her shoulder, some for Agustin, but also because the scent of cigarette smoke on Vangie's sweater reminded her of what she had walked away from.

Lola and Vangie finally went out for the lunches they'd been talking about for years. Usually, they went to Luby's on Saturdays. They both liked the cafeteria selection and they could stay as long as they wanted to. Vangie was always introducing Lola to her bowling friends she'd see at the restaurant. She and her husband, Beto, were on a men's and women's league that played every Wednesday night. When Vangie would introduce her as Lola, and not Mrs. Perez, it felt as if she were trying to pass for someone she'd met once many years earlier. It took some convincing for Lola to finally accept Vangie's invitation to come watch her bowl. She sat at a table on the upper level, so she could see all thirty lanes at once. Half the lanes were reserved for league play and half were for regular play. The bowling alley was louder than she ever imagined it would be. She found a new world in the thunder of the smashing pins, the musical notes coming from the pinball machines, the laughter of kids running around tables, the mournful sound of Freddy Fender's voice on the jukebox, the click-clack-click of the Foosball, and the crackling intercom that told everyone Cande's nachos were ready and getting cold.

She saw some of the same women Vangie had introduced her to at lunch, and now they came up between games and introduced her to their friends. There was an Alice and a Dora and a Linda and an Edith and a Dolly and a Terri, and so many others that she couldn't remember who was who. No, she'd never bowled, she kept having to tell all these new people. They looked at her as if she had told them she'd never been with a man.

"Do you want to try it?" Vangie asked her after the league play ended.

"Ay, no." Lola waved her away.

"Why?"

"Ya estoy muy vieja, Vangie."

"Lola, you're only two years older than me."

"Yeah, but you . . ."

"Come on, I'll show you how. You can quit if you don't like it."

Vangie pulled her out of her seat and brought her down to the floor. Lola stood next to Vangie and followed her motions. It was one, two, three, four steps and release the ball. Vangie held Lola's left hand and showed her how far back to swing her arm. All she had to do was aim for the little arrows on the floor. Holding Vangie's ball made her feel as if she were somehow being disloyal to Agustin, worse than if she had been carrying another man's urine in a glass bottle. Lola knocked down nine pins with her first throw. She picked up the spare on her second throw, and as fast as the number seven pin slammed into the back panel, she was hooked. She had strikes on her fifth and eighth frames. A month later she joined the Rio Grande Valley Women's League and played for De Luna Lumber Supply. On the back of her team shirt a giant hammer came smashing down on ten bowling pins that were running away with horror on their faces.

Lola had started bowling with a fourteen-pound ball she bought at the local pro shop. It was a plain black rubber ball that cost her $40. She still remembered how they took special care measuring her fingers for the holes and how it felt as if she were being fitted for an expensive piece of jewelry. She was happy now that she'd stored her old ball in the cuartito, next to the washer and dryer. This was the ball she'd be using for league play that night.

She spent the afternoon cleaning up the house and putting everything back in its place. Time passed quickly, until she got distracted looking at the old photos in the hatbox. Some of the pictures were more than forty years old. She found one taken in April 1947, when she and Agustin were honeymooning in Monterrey. They had spent the afternoon making love in their hotel room and that evening decided to go for a stroll. In the distance, they spotted an old man struggling to carry his large camera stand through the jardín. Lola waited while Agustin haggled with the photographer for twenty minutes. Agustin had offered him half the standard price. The old man kept saying it was unjust that he would be making only a few pesos for his services. His family had to eat, too. Agustin told him he would be making even less if he continued to be so terco about his price. Lola tried to help by saying she'd put in the extra pesos, but Agustin hushed her and said he would handle it. When he grabbed Lola's hand so they could walk away, the old man gave in. Agustin squeezed her hand and smiled to let her know he'd been planning it that way all along. In the photo, the newlyweds stood with their backs to a lit water fountain. Lola held a bouquet of flowers that Agustin had borrowed from a young man whose girlfriend hadn't shown up yet. Agustin gripped his new bride around her slender waist. She wore the nervous smile of a young woman who has just realized that she's boarded the wrong train.

Lola arrived at the bowling alley earlier than usual. She wanted to get comfortable with the old ball before everyone showed up. The manager was working behind the counter, and after he heard what happened, he let her borrow a pair of shoes on the house. She stopped by the pro shop and bought the same kind of wrist brace she had before. It took only a few frames for her to find her rhythm with the ball. The lanes had been conditioned that morning for the beginning of league play. She bowled a 174 on her first practice game.

Word spread quickly about Lola's cherry red ball. It seemed that she spent half the night answering questions about the break-in. She was having a hard time concentrating on her game. The loss of her ball sank in when her friends said how sorry they were about what had happened. The other ladies on the De Luna team were expecting her to score high for them. For most of the women, this was a social hour, a time to leave their husbands with the kids and go out with the girls. There was always talk going back and forth among the different teams. Lola joined in when they were just sitting around, but during the game she played to win.

She managed to pull it together in the second game and started knocking down some strikes. Between frames she kept to herself and let her teammates chat with one another. She thought about the teenager. She saw him laughing at her on the other side of the fence. He was slouching with his pants hanging low since he never ate anything besides other people's bananas. And he had a smirk on his face because he'd taken something that was hers and there was nothing an old woman could do about it. She put her anger into the release of the black ball. Her power rolled, spun, and hooked down sixty feet of maple wood until she found the perfect place to let out her frustration.

Her last game was her best. The bowling alley grew quiet each time she lined up with the ball. She had strikes in the first, second, and fourth frames. By then she'd forgotten about the teenager. She still wanted her ball back. It was hers and she'd paid enough for it, but she also knew it was just a ball. The important thing was that she was bowling a little better now. The ball hooked as if it were being pulled along a wire that extended from the foul line to the pocket. It was only the first week of the league, but she played as though it were the last. She had a strike on the tenth frame. On the bonus frame, she split the seven and ten pins and barely missed picking up the spare. Her final score was a 244. De Luna held on to second place, just behind Fernie's Pest Control.

Lola and Vangie stayed to have some beers with the rest of the team. One of the ladies commented that Lola must be color-blind because she had scored almost as many strikes with her black ball as she had with the cherry red one. The rest of the ladies laughed. Lola smiled, but she worried about how long it would take to really get her game back. She spent the next few weeks practicing and playing in the league. Afterward, she'd linger in front of the pro shop and gaze at the new bowling balls inside the glass case. At home she had several dog-eared catalogs with the latest models, but she couldn't make up her mind which, if any, to buy, so she decided to wait.

Two months passed before Lola regained her old form. It happened one night during league play when she scored a 284, a personal best. The black ball seemed to find a groove on the lane, and the strikes and spares just kept coming. Vangie and the other ladies stayed to have a beer after the last game, but Lola said she was tired. Next time, she told them. Lola drove down International and stared past the occasional headlights on the road. She thought about how well she had bowled that night and how her game had improved over the past few weeks. She felt that maybe she should've stayed for one beer. Her friends would be at the bowling alley for a while. Lola considered turning the car around, but she was already close to home. She decided instead to stop at the Jiffy-Mart to buy a six-pack. There were so many beers to choose from; she spent a few minutes opening and closing the refrigerator doors until she picked up a six-pack of Pearl Light. She walked to the counter with her fingers looped through the plastic ring holder. It took a while to get the clerk's attention because he was watching a boxing match on a mini-TV. "¡Chíngatelo!" he yelled from his wooden stool. She had to wait for the end of the round to buy her beer.

Lola placed the six-pack in the front seat of the car and pulled out of the parking lot. She had driven less than a block when she thought she saw the teenager walking in the direction of the store. Even in the dark, she recognized him walking the same cocky way he had in the alley with her bowling bag.

Lola turned the car around and drove back to the Jiffy-Mart. The teenager was about to reach the entrance when she stepped in front him. Her shoulders were back and her chin was up, but he was still a foot taller. She grabbed him by the shoulder and was surprised at the strength she felt in his arm.

"I want my ball."

"What are you talking about, grandma?"

"Tú fuiste. You stole it from my house. I saw you. I remember."

"You didn't see nothing, okay?" He yanked his arm back and leaned into Lola's face, close enough to kiss her. "And if you're smart, you'll keep your mouth shut."

His eyes were glassy and he smelled like the solution they used to condition the lanes.

"Give me back my ball."

"Shit, I already told you, I don't have your ball."

"Did you sell it?"

"Like I said, I don't know nothing about nothing."

"Le voy a hablar a la policía."

"And what? You want me to get all scared? Call them, there's the pay phone. I'll be cruising before they even get here."

"Just give me my ball."

"You're crazy, grandma." He shoved her aside and walked into the store.

Lola walked back to her car. From behind the steering wheel, she could see him standing at the back of the store, flipping through a magazine. He looked up between pages to see if she'd picked up the phone. All she wanted was her ball. If he gave it back, she wouldn't even report him. She thought about calling from her house, but she knew he'd be gone by the time the police arrived. She wished she'd never stopped at the store or seen the teenager walking down the dark street. Now she couldn't turn away. She couldn't let him walk away a second time. Her only chance was to call from the store's pay phone.

She opened the trunk of the car and unzipped her bag. She slipped on her wrist brace and pulled it snug around the palm of her hand. As she walked into the store, the black ball felt as if it were a part of her arm. The clerk was still shouting for his boxer to knock out the other guy. "¡Chíngatelo!" he kept yelling. The teenager stood at the end of the long aisle. He was laughing at something he'd seen in the magazine. Lola stepped back as far as she could. The tiles on the floor were white with tiny specks of red and green. The aisle was wider than a bowling lane. She locked her gaze on the teenager. She concentrated as she took her one, two, three, four steps and released the black ball down the aisle. The rumble started low and grew louder with each second. The ball stayed centered as it shot past the shelves of dishwashing liquid, detergent, oven cleaners, aluminum foil, diapers, pacifiers, formula mix, aspirin, cough syrup, cold and flu medicine, and then found its target: Strike!

Acknowledgments

Where would I be without you?

My father taught me how to work. My mother gave me faith. My big sister, Sylvia, and my cuñado, Jones, backed me up. Toni and Idoluis guided me with sound advice. Cindy walked with me one cold February morning in New York. Others called just to remind me I still had family and friends: Noel, Stephanie, David, Jason, Rene, Celeste, Nick, Scotty, DVH, and Jaime. Tío Nico inspired me to find my own stories. Tío Hector held the floor in our living room. Don Américo Paredes set the record straight and cleared a trail for the rest of us. Dago answered my letter and started me down this road. Dorothy Barnett read week after week and believed. David Rice agreed to look at this stranger's work. My tíos from Belton, Missouri, Imelda and Milton, stood in as my second parents. Matt, Josh, Jarod, and José listened while I first told some of these stories at Joe's Place. Victor Garcia and Tony Zavaleta filled in the details when my memory couldn't. El señor Garrido me dio las palabras. Lisa Marie spread the word to anyone who would stand still long enough. TZ sacrificed part of his honeymoon. Los Garcias y los Sassers opened their homes to me. Dylan and Flaco waited patiently for me to stop typing. Richard Abate never stopped asking if he could see the manuscript. Reagan Arthur and everyone at Little, Brown followed me home to Brownsville. And Cristal showed me the good that comes from love and patience.

A Note on the Type

The text of this book was set in Sabon, a typeface designed by Jan Tschichold (1902–74), a book designer and calligrapher, in the mid-1960s. Although he was a modernist and advocate of the Bauhaus style, his work as a book designer led him to create Sabon based on the early-sixteenth-century types of Claude Garamond. This classic and elegant typeface is now one of the most widely used in book design for its beauty and legibility.

The display type of this book is set in Weiss, designed by Emil Weiss (1875–1943), another book designer, in 1931. Weiss studied and admired the work of the classic type designers but was able to design and cut fonts for the then new technology of mechanically set type, making his work classic yet fresh and contemporary-looking.